Desperate Lives

Desperate Lives

**A Serialized Novel by
Wesley Adams and Daphne McGee**

Book 3 of the Soap Opera Inspired Story Collection
Series Created by Gary Brin

Episodes 1-4

Standish Press

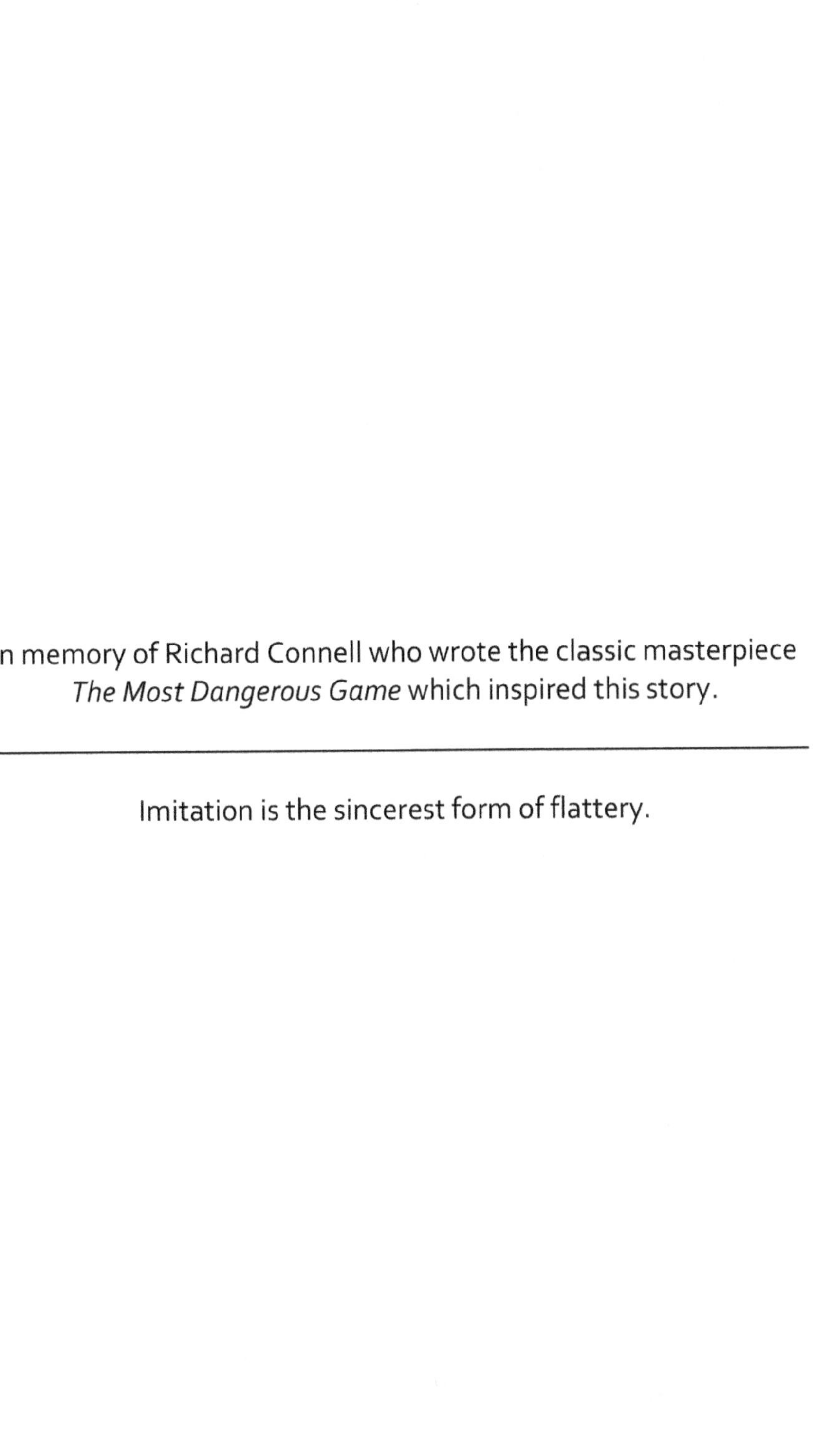

In memory of Richard Connell who wrote the classic masterpiece
The Most Dangerous Game which inspired this story.

Imitation is the sincerest form of flattery.

Contents

Intro 11

Prologue 13

A Brief Look at the First Episode 16

Episode 1 Ship of Fools 17

A Brief Look at the Second Episode 42

Episode 2 Desperate Lives 43

A Brief Look at the Third Episode 68

Episode 3 Edge of the World 69

A Brief Look at the Final Episode 94

Episode 4 End Games 95

About the Series Creator 116

Intro

This is an episodic reimagining of the classic story by Richard Connell which was first published in 1924. Nevertheless this version is not meant to be considered an official sequel. It is its own story with its own unique style that doesn't necessarily conform to previous versions—whether the 1924 print edition or the classic 1932 (*The Most Dangerous Game*) and 1945 (*A Game of Death*) film versions from RKO Pictures. Though the storyline in this edition isn't a completely original endeavor—this version spins an entirely new serialized plot incorporating present-day events and existence of modern technology that was worked into its script-like episodic storylines—blending fact and fiction into possible reality as the original story previously did in 1924.

This book, using some of the storylines from Richard Connell's 1924 masterpiece was created as a serialized inspired episodic novel written specifically to continue similarly formatted themes from long-ago daytime dramas as well as still-beloved prime-time soap classics—but with mature adult storylines added. Nevertheless despite the connections to Connell's novel, *Desperate Lives* was specifically written to resemble a filmed YouTube web series and though it occasionally imitates traditional classic soap operas to a certain extent—it was written with the intention that it's playing to a visual audience and therefore will emulate a script format (without camera angle directions) rather than the usual storytelling methods displayed in popular full-length novels such as *Peyton Place* by Grace Metalious and *Celebrity* by Thomas Thompson. Each episode of the novels in this series were written in a brief span of 6-12 days or less and shouldn't be confused with being great literature by any means whatsoever. The goal of this series is simply to mimic episodes of modern-day daytime soap operas or entertaining YouTube web series dramas—by creating visual entertainment on a printed page—and not to create a literary masterpiece.

The storyline in *Desperate Lives* takes place approximately one year after the events in *Glass Owl* wrapped up and nearly a century after an incident involving a big game hunter and a Russian madman ended abruptly. Several characters from *Glass Owl* are featured in this book as part of the present story.

Gary Brin
Series Creator

In an effort to have an accurate portrayal of the dialogue used for the *Soap Opera Inspired Story Collection Series* people were anonymously observed in shopping malls, schools, places of employment, and on public streets in order to capture a definitive portrayal of how people of various ages and cultures interacted and talked to each other when they thought no one was listening. While some select dialogue was exaggerated for dramatic purposes when needed—the manner and tone of which people were observed speaking to each other in casual and private conversations is accurate. Exact wording was not copied verbatim for the most part, but the way certain types of topics and conversations are addressed by characters in this serialized series is based on actual situations that were observed over a period of several dozen years.

Prologue

1

1924

The man fought his way through the jungle for several hours. His mind is clear as he feels his way along the path leading away from the mansion perched above jagged cliffs. He knows that he's going in the right direction but still he feels nervous knowing he's the prey and not the hunter. His main goal is simple—put plenty of distance between himself and the crazed hunter who has been stalking him. But as he plunges along the thick wooded area, panic begins to gnaw at him as he thinks of what lays before him—knowing that it will ultimately bring him face to face again with the sea of which he just came after an error in bad judgment suddenly changed his life forever.

2

He looks at his hands and touches his face lightly, fully aware of the welts caused by the branches along the path. He knows it's insanity to blunder through the dense woods at night, but he has no choice in the matter after the threat from the unstable man who calls himself Zaroff was made clear when he refused to hunt one of the unfortunate shipwreck victims being held against their will until they are needed to play the sick game Zaroff had devised in order to keep himself amused. He wants to take a break and rest but knows he has to be vigilant. He notices a huge tree with a wide trunk and extended branches. He climbs up, careful not to leave any evidence that could be noticed later. Rest comes easily but his mind continues to work feverishly. Toward morning, the cry of a startled bird focuses his attention immediately, and through a mass of thick leaves he notices someone approaching cautiously from a hundred yards away.

3

General Zaroff makes his way through the dense jungle as his eyes focuses on the ground before him. He stops suddenly at a tree and drops to his knees to study the ground with determined precision. The hunter shakes his head several times slightly puzzled at the intelligence of his newest prey. His eyes leave the ground and travels inch by inch up the tree—but then suddenly without warning he turns and carelessly walks away, back along the trail he had come as if someone has called him suddenly. A few birds can be heard over the noise of wind blowing loudly.

4

The man slides down from the tree, and takes off again into the jungle, only to realize too late he's being followed by General Zaroff once more. So intent is the hunter on his stalker that he instantly notices a trap set earlier in the morning by his prey and stops cold. As the skilled hunter stands there pondering his next move, the prey silently takes off again through the thick underbrush of the interior of the island and into a swamp nearby. His foot sticks to the thick muck as he comes upon the area but with a violent effort the prey tears his foot loose and looks around as if not sure of his next move. Then an idea comes to him and he began to dig furiously. With his fingers rapidly moving, he weaves a crude carpet of weeds and a few branches—and with it he covers the mouth of the hole he just dug. A perfect trap for one of the dogs if they so choose to dare. Then, with sweat, and aching with extreme weariness, the prey begins his sly gameplay. Except now the prey is the hunter and the hunter becomes the prey.

5

On a ridge nearby the man climbs a tree and watches as a moving figure can be seen followed by a group of dogs. The hounds stop abruptly as the man uses the opportunity to double back on the trail in order to confuse the dogs. Up ahead he sees the shore of the raging sea about ten yards away—and across the cove he notices the outline of the mansion. He leaps into the sea seconds later. The man swims furiously and finally reaches the jagged cliffs. Several minutes later he stands at the entrance.

6
Game Over

The man silently looks at his prey and grins. He was once the hunter but a mistake has changed events and now the man who had been hunted was set to hunt himself. The gun lay between them in the darkened room and it took a split second to grab for it. There is a struggle and then a single gunshot rings out in the damp night. As the shot rings out, the silence that had permeated the late evening comes to an end. There is a loud cry and then one of them lies dying before the other. From outside the loud barking of dogs can be heard over the sound of waves crashing against the side of the cliff beneath the mansion.

A Brief Look at the First Episode

A seemingly peaceful excursion to the Amazon for a diverse group of people suddenly turns into a tragedy as events unfold concerning the sordid personal life of an unfaithful wife and her much-older husband in the middle of the Caribbean Sea.

Episode 1
Ship of Fools

This serialized variation of the classic 1924 novella *The Most Dangerous Game* by Richard Connell picks up a century after the original concluded with a surprise ending.
Certain events and characters mentioned previously in the original story will figure into the present storyline.

1
Reynolds Estate
St. Thomas
United States Virgin Islands

"I'm going—deal with it already."

Armand Bell slams the kitchen door shut and heads to the driveway as his mother Nancy Reynolds follows in a panic.

"It's dangerous—your father *is* dangerous."

Armand stops and turns to look at his mother. They share an uneasy moment of silence. He looks back at the house.

"Dad isn't dangerous—he just takes lots of risks. Lives on the edge—he's that kind of guy—OK—so quit freaking."

"It wasn't my fault—I had to leave."

Nancy grabs her son's arm.

"I divorced your father because he didn't know how to stop getting into trouble. He's been in jail more times than I care to count—and now this *bizarre* trip to South America."

Armand mockingly rolls his eyes.

"I'm nineteen—I can think for myself."

He unlocks the car door.

"Besides, this will be a good time to get to know dad better—after what happened with—of which you know."

Nancy seems stung by the comment from her son.

"I *had* to leave your father—the incident in Tasmania was the last straw. You almost died—such dangerous animals."

Armand gets into his car as his mother suddenly reaches out to grab the door before he can shut it. She sighs loudly.

"This will only be a distraction from your classes."

"Nice try mother—but classes don't start for six weeks."

He smirks broadly.

"I'll be fine—like quit worrying—I'm not a little boy—so stop treating me like I'm ten—quite annoying actually."

"Please be careful—remember what I said about your father Armand—think before you act—just be safe—*please*."

"See you in four weeks."

He pulls out of the driveway and waves. As he drives away Nancy seems worried and quickly pulls out her cell phone.

2

New York City

"Uh-huh—got it—like bring back a story worth printing for your crummy tabloid no matter what the hell I have to do."

Scott Malone glances at his cell phone.

"Bet you didn't think I'd take the job—but I will."

He looks out at the city below.

"And I'll hold you to the promised payout."

Roland Parker suddenly sits up and leans forward from his desk looking annoyed. He watches Scott's reaction and sighs.

Page 18

"This is your last chance Malone. Had enough of your failures to last a lifetime—and after what happened last month with that actor—I'm about ready to wash my hands of you."

Scott rolls his eyes and sighs loudly.

"Hey—how was I supposed to know Jared Isling was gay?"

Roland leans back in his chair.

"Like how hard could it be? The man always seemed to have a "best buddy" around all the time—even when he was supposed to be dating that actress from that crappy Netflix show that just got axed last year—and then they split and rumors started to fly—suddenly the "best buddy" got deep-sixed."

Roland picks up his cell phone.

"Like I said—last try Malone—this time I mean it."

Roland watches as Scott turns to leave.

"I'm not kidding. I want you to take the next flight out to the Virgin Islands—be on that goddamned boat when Bell pulls out of port—no more excuses—not even one—zero. Got it?"

Scott turns to look at Roland again with a smirk.

"Yeah—I got the message loud and clear."

He leaves seconds later.

3
Marlowe Driveway
St. Thomas
United States Virgin Islands

Myles Stephenson throws two pieces of luggage into the backseat of his car and slams the door shut. From the corner of his eye he sees Jennifer Marlowe coming toward him.

"Do you know when you'll be back from your trip?"

Myles sighs and looks at Jennifer with a knowing grin.

"Four weeks—I think."

Jennifer slides her arms around his waist.

"I'll miss you."

Myles grins broadly.

"I take what happened earlier left an impact?"

Page **19**

Jennifer laughs.

"What do you think?"

They kiss passionately.

"Call me OK?"

"I will—promise I will."

They kiss briefly and then again more passionately.

4
New York City

Scott slams the door shut behind him and begins making reservations for a flight as he walks down the hallway. He seems slightly stressed as he slowly steps into an elevator.

"I swear—Parker needs to get laid."

He smirks and rolls his eyes knowingly.

"Speaking of which—could use a quickie myself."

He licks his lips sensuously.

"I think Marisa Boynton is due one last visit from her main guy—she and I need to get reacquainted—like seriously."

Scott begins dialing as he whistles loudly.

"Hope she's over what happened with Julie Carrington last week—like it wasn't really much of a big deal anyways."

The elevator opens.

5
Havensight Mall
St. Thomas
United States Virgin Islands

Armand grins broadly as he looks at the huge yacht up ahead. He shoves his hands into the front pockets of his Levi's and sighs as he causally walks through Havensight Mall and heads toward the docks. He stops suddenly at a pair of iron gates.

"Hope you like surprises dad."

He heads toward the entrance with a grin.

6
Bell Yacht
West Indian Company Dock
St. Thomas
United States Virgin Islands

Tristan Montgomery Bell sighs loudly.
"This time will be different."
He stands up and slowly walks to the window.
"No wicked distractions this time."
He turns to look at a wrinkled magazine lying on a desk nearby with a torn photo of a handsome man on the cover.

One Day Later

7
Bell Yacht
Somewhere in the Caribbean Sea

Loud sounds of intense lovemaking can be heard outside a door leading to a private cabin aboard a large luxury yacht.
"And you said."
The man laughs and pulls away from the woman. He smirks as he lies back in bed and sighs in satisfaction.
"Uh-huh—and you said you wouldn't give it up to me."
The woman glances at the man.
"What happens now?"
"What do you think?"
He winks at her.
"By the way my name is Myles Stephenson."
The woman seems nervous and sighs.
"Daphne—Daphne—no last name necessary."
She grabs her blouse.
"If my husband finds out—he'd never understand."
Myles laughs loudly.
"I won't tell."

He looks at his exposed penis.
"Hope you're on the pill."
Daphne Wade Bell rolls her eyes.
"What if I wasn't?"
Myles looks at his exposed penis again and laughs.
"Hope your husband is ready to be a *daddy*."
She seems upset.
"Am I just another notch on your bedpost Myles?"
Myles grins slyly.

8

Two men are sitting at the top of a stairwell glancing at a door to a closed suite several feet away. One of them sighs.
"Can you believe that guy?"
Jason Carson shakes his head disapprovingly as he looks over at his friend Kyle Bennett. He clenches his fist.
"Frigging creep—son of a fucking bitch—of all the people he could fuck on this yacht today—he had to target *her*."
He sighs loudly.
"She's a married woman for Christ sakes."
"When did you become such a prude—especially with your mouth being so quick to spout filthy four-letter words?"
Jason shoots Kyle a nasty look.
"Hey—the old man may not be much to look at—but that doesn't mean he should be played by the likes—of *him*."
Kyle rolls his eyes.
"Stephenson didn't have to twist her arm too hard if I recall—they hooked-up just ten minutes after they met."
Jason shrugs and hesitantly nods his head.
"OK—*Daphne Bell is a whore*—but that still doesn't mean Stephenson is a prince—he uses women like tissue paper."
Kyle nods in agreement and rolls his eyes.
"No one cares."
Jason reaches over to shove Kyle.
"Think you're really funny—don't you?"

Page **22**

Kyle gestures with his hand and sighs loudly.

"Nope—but let's get real for a change—when was the last time you had a date with a chick—a real one—not one of those freaky online things where she turns out to be 75 years old."

At that moment they hear the suite door open and see Myles tucking his T-shirt into his faded Levi's. He grins.

"Hey Guys."

He notices their harsh glares and shrugs. Behind him Daphne emerges from the cabin and she realizes they have an audience. She looks away as if more scared than ashamed.

"Nice day—isn't it?"

Myles watches for a reaction. But there's none. They walk away without saying another word. Jason turns to look at Kyle.

"I should say something—seriously I should."

Kyle grabs Jason by the arm. He seems angry.

"Not one word—do you hear me? If old man Bell finds out his sweet young wife has been playing house with the hired help—sampling his wares—he might just take up one of his guns and kill the slimy bastard—want a murder on your watch?"

"Bell should be told his wife is a cheap slut."

"No way—really bad idea—he'll snap for sure."

Kyle looks at Jason cautiously.

"You and I are just here to guide that old man through the South American jungle—we didn't sign on to keep tabs on his wife—especially when it comes to a creep like Stephenson."

Jason angrily clenches his fists.

"That damned slug has no class whatsoever—he deserves to suffer for how he treats women. He needs to be outed."

He wipes sweat from his brow.

"That man has no shame when it comes to women—heard he bedded over 1000—broke up countless marriages without a second thought—one of which was that movie star and her jock husband—the one who was chased by dinosaurs in that really bad movie that came out about ten years ago—heard the dude walked in on his wife and Stephenson doing the deed—freaked out royally and lost his mind right after—shot up the place."

A look of disgust comes across his face.

"Uh-huh—Bell should have been told beforehand about Stephenson. Yeah—he may have globe-trotted all over Africa with that damned camera of his—but his rep—so shameful."

"Didn't he kill himself?"

"No—his wife called the cops when things got out of control and they carted the poor sucker away to the booby hatch—I think the sad sap is still there in a padded room."

"Tough break—guess his brilliant sports career is over?"

"You think?"

He wipes sweat from his brow again and sighs.

"Fine—whatever—I won't say a word."

Kyle nods in agreement.

9

"Do you think they know?"

Myles grins and looks back at the two men.

"Is the Pope Catholic?"

He kisses her on the cheek. She pulls away. He seems confused by her cold behavior. He smirks and tries to sneak another quick kiss. She pushes him away immediately.

"What's the matter?"

He laughs.

"What's with the cold shoulder?"

"This was a mistake—if Tristan found out—oh God."

"Why would Tristan Montgomery Bell give a damn if you and I hooked-up in my cabin for an hour? Is he your dad?"

"Tristan is not my father—he's my *husband*. I married him just over a year ago—he and I met in Sydney, Australia."

Myles reacts with a look of panic on his face.

10

Tristan looks closely at the map in front of him again and then turns to look at his assistant Cooper Johnston curiously.

"So, according to this old map, there's supposed to be an island somewhere out there—uncharted and uninhabited?"

Cooper nods.

"Uh-huh—from what I heard."

Tristan sighs.

"I know these waters like the back of my hand—and I've never seen an island this far out from the Virgin Islands."

Cooper points to the map.

"This map is from National Geographic."

Tristan shrugs.

"So?"

Cooper rolls his eyes noticing Tristan's expression.

"There should be an island out there."

They look at each other.

"You're not making any sense."

Cooper sighs.

"According to the stories I've heard from a few of my friends on St. Thomas—there *is* an island southeast of the Virgin Islands but all records of its existence have been mysteriously erased from modern maps—even from Google Earth from what I heard—no trace anywhere to find whatsoever—none."

Tristan shrugs and looks at the map again.

"How can you erase an island from Google Earth?"

Cooper runs his fingers through his hair.

"They didn't say."

Tristan looks at his watch.

"I've heard enough of this drivel."

He slams his fist against the steering wheel.

"Make yourself useful Cooper—go find Wesley Mayfield right now—he and I need to talk seriously—like ASAP."

Cooper nods again.

"Going to ask him about Google Earth?"

Tristan pushes Cooper.

"Yeah—that's right—I'm going to ask questions about something that sounds like nonsense—uh-huh—for sure."

Cooper backs away nervously.

"I was just telling you what I heard."

They look at each other.

"An island can't just disappear from a map—especially from Google Earth—and most certainly not from those maps National Geographic puts out every couple of years. Got it?"

Cooper shrugs and nervously turns to leave.

11

Armand leans against the railing and looks out to sea. He seems bored as he turns around and looks at his watch.

"Not quite what I expected—not at all."

"And me?"

Armand turns to see a young woman giving him a curious stare. He grins broadly at the sight of the beautiful woman.

"Am I what you expected?"

He laughs nervously. She notices.

"And you'd be?"

"Serena St. John."

She leans toward him and whispers in his ear.

"Nice body—hope you're straight?"

Armand smirks.

"Like an arrow."

Serena grins and strokes Armand's arm.

"FYI straight guy—I like men with experience."

Armand gives her a sly look.

"I've got plenty of experience with women—a virgin I'm not—been around the block quite a few times and then some."

Serena looks down at his snug-fitting jeans.

"Exactly how big are you?"

Serena traces her finger down the front of his Levi's and begins unzipping the zipper. She glances back at him as she notices his swelling erection straining under the fabric.

"I can hold my own."

"How about we test that theory?"

He laughs as he slyly leers at her. She notices.

"Lead the way—but be warned."

She kisses Armand.

"You'd better not disappoint me. I take being slighted very seriously. I'm expecting you to rise to the occasion."

They kiss again.

12

"That old coot is your frigging husband? Why didn't you tell me before I stuck my dick into you—like this is seriously messed up—of all the stupid moves you could make?"

Daphne slaps Myles.

"How dare you blame me for this mess—if you hadn't insisted on us fucking we wouldn't have a problem now."

Myles runs his fingers through his hair.

"OK—OK—we're still in the clear."

Myles sighs loudly.

"No one knows anything happened between us."

Daphne glances over her shoulder.

"Are you sure about that?"

Myles looks where Daphne's nervous gaze is focused.

13

"You fucked a total stranger?"

"I couldn't help it—we did it in a stairwell."

Amanda Hardwick rolls her eyes.

"Better check for STDs."

Marlene Caswell sighs loudly.

"He's not a manwhore—he told me he just broke up with his longtime girlfriend last week—said she hurt him badly."

She strokes her cheek nervously.

"Said she cheated on him—he and I—he was so sweet."

Amanda grabs Marlene by the arm.

"Uh-huh—does Prince Charming have a name?"

Marlene shrugs knowingly.

"Myles—just like that Pilgrim guy **Myles Standish**."
Amanda seems about to explode.

14

"They wouldn't dare."
"You better hope those two clowns keep quiet."
She shakes her head.
"If Tristan even suspects you and I—things could get quite dangerous quickly. My husband has a terrible temper."
Daphne looks out to sea.
"That and he's an excellent shot."
Daphne leans against the railing and glances at Myles.
"It's not too late to head back to St. Thomas?"
He shrugs.
"Can't do it—I need the money."
They look at each other.
"We've just got to make sure those two idiot yoyos keep their traps shut—can't have them blabbing to the old man."
"We could throw them overboard before they spill—dead men can't tell tales. Who'd know any better after the fact?"
He grimaces.
"Yeah—*like* no."
Myles runs his fingers through his hair nervously.
"Let's see what's their deal first—everyone has a price."
"And if your plan doesn't work?"
"I'm not killing anybody."
Daphne grabs Myles by the arm.
"It could be your funeral?"
Myles casually glances at two scantily-clad women on the lower deck. Daphne turns away in disgust. She seems angry.
"*Like really*—our lives are in serious jeopardy of being deep-sixed tonight and you're thinking about your dick?"
Myles grins broadly.
"I'm a single guy—OK—deal."
He smirks and looks back at the two women.

Page 28

"Got to make friends—would be rude if I didn't mingle."

Seconds later he sprints down the stairs.

15

Wesley Mayfield watches as Tristan slowly closes the door behind him. He seems oddly nervous about something.

"Said you wanted to see me?"

They look at each other.

"If this is about the report you asked for earlier?"

Tristan wipes sweat from his brow.

"I need you to keep an eye on Cooper. Seems he thinks we're on *Amazing Race* or something—I don't need to deal with him having a troubling relapse of what happened in Kenya last year concerning that creepy incident with the park ranger."

"Will do—*anything else?*"

Tristan seems suddenly irritated.

"Find my wife—she and I need to talk—got to set a few ground rules before we reach port—especially after."

Wesley nods again and leaves. Tristan turns to look once more at the open ocean. He wrings his hands several times.

16

"Myles Stephenson—oh—*oh my God Marlene*—of all the single men you could've messed around with yesterday."

Marlene shakes her head.

"I met him at a gift shop just before we boarded and one thing led to another in the stairwell—so shoot me already."

Marlene looks at Amanda suspiciously.

"*Wait*—how do you his name? I didn't tell you his name? Did you? OMG—he fucked you too? You and Myles fucked?"

Amanda turns away.

"I couldn't help myself. He was just so handsome and sexy—like a slightly younger version of **Alexander Skarsgard**."

Amanda licks her lips seductively.

"Yesterday morning at my hotel room—I thought he was a decent guy—gentle—but then I saw him making a play for Vicki de Hoya at the hotel bar minutes after he left my room."

Marlene seems shocked at the revelation.

"*Vicki*—as in Victoria de Hoya—the coffee heiress—how could he think she's—she's like fifty—*and* like so ancient."

Amanda rolls her eyes.

"Obviously he's a dog who will fuck anything."

"I hate men—hate them so much."

"Sign me up for that club."

Marlene looks around at the room.

"OK—maybe I don't hate men—especially cute men. But I hate Myles Stephenson—filthy piece of sleaze—so gross."

Amanda nods in agreement.

17
New York City

Roland leans back in his chair and sighs loudly. He looks at the cell phone in his hand and seems irritated. He shrugs.

"I hear what you're saying Thomas—but I can't come to Portland until next week—got too much on my plate here."

He rolls his eyes.

"I don't know the guy you're talking about—he's not one of my people. I promised you I wouldn't do any stories about the events surrounding your adopted daughter's mental issues."

He gestures with his hand.

"Nevertheless, I recall telling you to get her some help about four years ago—which you ignored. Jennifer Parker needed help long before she went on a killing spree in Marble Hills."

He gestures again and sighs.

"Uh-huh—I'll be in touch shortly."

He shuts off his cell phone and slowly stands up.

"I wonder who's snooping around Portland looking for a story about my brother's late deranged stepdaughter."

He glances at the window.

18

Daphne notices Jason standing at the far end of the yacht looking out to sea. He faces her as she approaches him.

"It's not what it seemed."

Jason rolls his eyes.

"Is that so—seems to me it was exactly what it appeared to be—you and that piece of trash fooling around on the sly."

Daphne sighs loudly.

"Are you going to tell Tristan?"

Jason looks away.

"*Well*, are you?"

Jason turns to face Daphne with a cold stare.

"I don't know yet."

Daphne grabs Jason by the arm.

"You can't tell."

Jason angrily pulls free of Daphne's grip.

19

Myles glances at the two women in his bed. He grins broadly as he begins kissing Laura Wiley passionately.

"Hope you're on the pill."

Laura begins moaning as Myles penetrates her.

"If my mother could see me now—giving it up to a guy I just met a few minutes ago—what was your name again?"

Myles laughs.

"Myles—name's Myles."

He grins.

"Not interested in a commitment."

Myles looks over at the other woman lying on the bed besides them and gives her a sly grin. He smirks knowingly.

"Are you ready for me too?"

Diana Munroe nods as he licks his lips.

20

Armand pulls on his boxer briefs and turns to look at Serena lying on the bed. He walks over to her and grins.
"Well?"
Serena sits up in bed.
"Not bad."
"That means good—scale of 1 to 10?"
Serena smirks.
"I'm still deciding."
"Hey?"
Armand leans over to kiss Serena.

21

Daphne stares at the huge expanse of ocean and sighs loudly. Her fingers grip the rail tightly as she shakes her head.
"How could I have been so incredibly stupid?"
"Who are you talking to?"
She spins around to see Tristan looking at her.
"Is everything all right?"
"Why do you ask?"
"You seem tense Daphne—what's wrong?"
Daphne shakes her head.
"If this is about our upcoming trip—rest assured those crazy stories about monsters is fiction—no such things exist."
Daphne seems uneasy.
"I'm not worried about giant lizards."
Tristan nervously pulls Daphne toward him.
"Then what is it?"
He looks into her eyes.
"I know something is wrong—is it us?"
Daphne shrugs.
"No—it's me."
She pulls away from Tristan and looks out at the ocean.
"I have to tell you something."

An awkward moment of silence slips by.

"What is it Daphne? I thought we'd come so far after what happened two months ago—thought that was long over."

"We have—*I have.*"

Tristan gives Daphne an odd look. She shrugs.

"I did—but things have happened."

Daphne faces Tristan again.

"I wish."

She hesitates.

"I wish I was the wife you deserve."

Tristan pulls Daphne toward him again.

"What's going on Daphne?"

Daphne pushes Tristan away from her.

"I—I just seem to make things worse no matter how hard I try not to screw up—you deserve so much more Tristan."

Tristan sighs loudly.

"Is it me—did I do something?"

"No—I did. I'm the only one to blame—as always."

Tristan seems confused by the comment.

22

A figure walks toward a door and opens it. Enters the room—and places a photograph on top of a desk—then leaves the room seconds later—silently pulling the door shut.

23

"What about the other girls I saw you with earlier?"

Myles grins slyly and seems to hide a smirk.

"What about them?"

Sandra King looks at Myles curiously.

"I don't like being second."

Myles laughs.

"You're not second Sandra—OK—I don't do seconds—like never—so just let us enjoy a few possibilities—and positions."

He laughs again.
"Or do I have to beg?"
Myles smirks.
"Might give me a complex—and a visit to a shrink?"
Sandra reaches out to kiss Myles.
"You're just *too* charming for us girls to resist."
Myles winks.
"I'm counting on that."
He leads her down the hallway.

24

"Can I speak with you?"
Daphne turns around to see Cooper a few feet away from where she and Tristan are standing. He seems really upset.
"Can't it wait?"
Cooper shakes his head.
"No."
Tristan gives Cooper a curious stare and slowly turns to look at Daphne. He notices her reaction at being interrupted.
"I'll only be a minute."
"Fine—I'll wait."
Tristan seems confused at Daphne's reaction and slowly turns to face Cooper as Daphne appears to get more agitated.
"Well—what is so damned important?"
Daphne leans against the railing as she watches Tristan talk with Cooper. He seems really upset about something.
"I wish there was another way."
Cooper pulls out something from his jacket pocket. He gives it to Tristan. Daphne strains to hear what they are talking about as Tristan suddenly becomes enraged seconds later.

25

Sandra seems upset as she watches Myles casually tuck his T-shirt into his faded Levi's and glances at her once more.

Page 34

"Much thanks for the ride."
Sandra sits up in bed.
"When can I see you again?"
"I'll let you know."
"But I just let you—is that it?"
Myles seems irritated by Sandra's needy behavior.
"I'll call you tomorrow."
He leaves without saying goodbye.

26

Jason walks aimlessly along the hallway as he shakes his head several times and sighs loudly. He stops suddenly.
"Maybe I won't have to tell?"
He sighs again.
"Maybe the old man will put two and two together?"
He clenches his fist.
"Or someone else will tell him?"
He hears a noise and turns around in a panic.
"What the fuck?"
He seems enraged.

27

Myles grins broadly as he scans the horizon. He seems happy. Ahead of his gaze he sees a faint outline of land.
"An island—must be a mirage—I don't recall any islands this far out from St. Thomas—definitely seeing things."
"Seeing what?"
He turns to see Wesley standing a few feet away.
"Thought I saw an island?"
Wesley seems confused at the comment.
"Only open ocean all the way to South America."
Myles looks again at the horizon and sees nothing. He turns back to face Wesley. He rubs his eyes briefly.
"Uh-huh—nothing out there."

Wesley looks at his watch several times.

"Bell will probably want to talk with you before we reach Brazil—he likes to keep close tabs on his crew—be aware."

Myles nods.

"Thanks for the heads up."

Wesley sighs.

"Just don't get into trouble."

Myles gives Wesley an odd stare.

"Wasn't planning to be a dick?"

"Good—keep it that way—certainly wouldn't want what happened with Ralph Fawcett a while back to happen again so soon after—such a mess to clean up—not fun—no way."

Myles grabs Wesley's arm.

"Bell hired Fawcett before he did me?"

Wesley nods.

"He did—fired him after he caught Fawcett and Daphne together in the pool house at his summer estate in Miami."

Myles lets go of Wesley's arm.

"Is that that happened?"

"Why do you ask?"

"Fawcett disappeared two months ago."

"So?"

"And you say this "event" happened a while back?"

Wesley seems annoyed.

"If you're going where I think you're going—don't—right after Fawcett got canned by Bell he got a job with some big travel outfit in northern Alaska—and it was there he disappeared—from what I heard Ralph Fawcett got trapped in a freak blizzard."

"I was just asking—chill OK?"

Wesley gives Myles a cold stare.

"You're a photographer—not one of the *Hardy Boys*. Stick to taking pictures—not minding other people's business."

Myles rolls his eyes.

"*Ouch*—quite harsh don't you think?"

"Don't fuck with me Stephenson—it's not too late to have you replaced—Brazil has plenty of qualified photographers."

Page **36**

"Good to know buddy."

Myles walks away as Wesley continues to stand there.

28
Coast Guard Headquarters
Miami

Brad McFadden slowly opens the door to his office and sighs loudly as he sees his young assistant sitting at his desk.

"I thought we went over the chair issue already?"

Casey Roberts grins broadly.

"Yeah—but when was the last time I listened?"

He stands up.

"I just got another report on that Caribbean issue."

Brad glances at the folder in Casey's hand.

"Just tell me the deal already."

Casey rolls his eyes.

"Four."

Brad walks toward where Casey is standing.

"How long ago since they were reported missing?"

"Two weeks."

He sighs.

"Richard and Liza Hamilton from Boston and their two teenage sons—not a single word from any of them since they were reported missing just outside the US Virgin Islands."

"Book me a flight."

Casey gestures at a nearby table.

"Done—you leave in one hour—45 minutes flat—should be in Charlotte Amalie by nightfall. Peter Zimmerman from the Virgin Islands Coast Guard is going to meet you at the airport there. He has a crew ready to take this to the next step."

Brad waves his hand.

"Forget what I said earlier about the chair."

"You said something earlier Brad? Oops—oh-oh I wasn't really listening—must have dozed off or something I guess."

Brad points his finger at Casey.

"We'll resume this topic when I get back."
Brad shakes his fist and leaves. Casey sighs loudly.
"Probably won't end well for the Hamiltons."
He glances nervously at the huge window in front of him.

29

Jason looks at his former son-in-law Harley Vanning with obvious hatred. He reaches out to grab the younger man by his shirt collar. Harley aggressively pushes Jason's hand away.
"What the fuck are you doing here?"
"Got to pay the bills don't I?"
Jason clenches his fists.
"Thought I made it clear you were to stay away from me and my family indefinitely—especially my daughter."
Harley rolls his eyes.
"Exactly how long are you going to hold a grudge over what happened between your precious daughter and me?"
Jason pushes Harley against the rail.
"You cheated on my daughter Vanning—and not just once either. Have you no shame? How could you think what you did was okay? She loved you—and you fucked it up royally."
Harley untangles himself from Jason's grip.
"You're a fucking loser—you treated my only daughter without a shred of respect—and then you had the nerve to say after the fact you were unhappy? Like really—what about my daughter? What about her? Goddamn you Vanning—when they found your name in the black book of that trashy madam who got busted for running a brothel out of the cellar at St. Mark's Church—that was the last straw. Fucking whore had four stars by your name—and we both know it wasn't because you were such a good listener. Damn near destroyed my daughter's sanity when she found out you had been screwing around with people like that. Get the frigging hell out of my sight this instant or else."
Harley nervously wrings his hands.
"I'm not going anywhere."

Page 38

They stare at each for a few seconds.

"Fuck off old man."

"I want you out of here the minute we get to Brazil."

Jason looks out to sea.

"Or I won't be responsible for what happens."

"Is that a threat I hear from you Carson?"

Jason looks out to sea again.

"Very deep waters out there—fatal accidents happen all the time. I'd think seriously about that fact if I were you."

"I'm not afraid."

"Then you're dumber than you look."

He turns to leave and looks back at Harley briefly.

"Have a nice day."

He smirks.

"Or may not—especially when you consider how deep the ocean in this part of the world happens to be—so deep."

Jason whistles as he heads down the hallway gleefully glancing back every now and then. Harley sighs loudly again.

"He wouldn't. He wouldn't dare."

Harley looks at the ocean in a distance.

30

Scott leans against the door as he looks at Sandra. She doesn't notice him standing there. He grins broadly.

"Going to the gym does a body good."

Sandra turns around to look at Scott. He smirks.

"Hey—noticed you working out from deck above—really liked what I saw so I came by—came by for a closer look."

Sandra rolls her eyes.

"Got any better lines? Oh-oh—I hear the 1980s calling you right about now—seem they want their cheesy line back."

Scott pretends to be insulted by her comment.

"Is that your way of telling me we aren't going to have dinner later? Such a shame if that's the case—like really."

"Why should I have dinner with you?"

Page **39**

"I'm a fun guy."

He winks slyly at her.

"In bed and on the dance floor—ask my exes if you don't believe me—I'm a seriously popular dude—especially when I'm not wearing pants—definitely could teach you a few things."

She glances at his corduroy jeans and winks.

"Bold talk from a guy with such bad lines initially."

Scott suddenly pulls Sandra towards him.

"So, how about it—dinner in an hour in my cabin—and then maybe some action between the sheets right after?"

Sandra rolls her eyes.

"I don't even know you?"

"One dinner is all it takes."

"What if I say no?"

Scott strokes Sandra's hair with his fingers.

"You won't."

He looks at his watch.

"I'm in cabin 7."

He continues to stroke her hair.

"And no—I don't have a current girlfriend."

Scott laughs.

"At least none I'd admit to."

He smiles slyly.

"But I'm open to the idea."

He laughs.

"A guy has the right to change his mind."

Seconds later Sandra watches as Scott walks away. She sighs several times and grabs a towel from a nearby rack.

31
Two Hours Later

Tristan enters his office and notices a photo lying on the floor next to his desk. He walks over and picks it up. He begins to shake as he realizes what he's watching. He drops the photo and clenches his fist angrily. He glances at the open door.

Page 40

"I'm going to kill him. No one disrespects me and lives to brag about it—how dare he play me for a fool. Fuck him."

He clenches his fists again.

"And to think I gave him a frigging job."

He looks at the horizon in a distance.

"Bastard probably thought he'd get away with it—well surprise asshole—the jig's up. Time you learned a lesson."

For a few seconds he remains deathly still.

"Can't let this slight go unpunished—got to even the score and make an impact. I'll make the bastard beg for mercy."

He walks over to the metal cabinet at the far end of his office and hastily begins turning the silver tumbler on the combination lock. He fingers tremble as the door swings open a few seconds later. He looks inside at a handgun lying on top of a thick stack of paperwork and flash drives. He sighs loudly.

"Fawcett disrespected me and ended up dead."

He grabs the handgun and looks at it.

"Uh-huh—got away with it too—quite easy if I do say so myself. Even his family bought that lame blizzard story."

He stops to look at the door.

"Second time around will be much easier."

He slides his fingers across the barrel.

"No one will miss him. It'll easily be believed that he fell overboard in a drunken stupor. Case closed instantly."

He heads to the door leaving the cabinet unlocked.

TO BE CONTINUED

A Brief Look at the Second Episode

Tristan angrily confronts the person he feels wronged him with a gun—leading to a tragic disaster for everyone on board the yacht headed to South America—resulting from the fallout caused by a mysterious photo left intentionally in Tristan's office earlier.

Episode 2
Desperate Lives

1
Bell Yacht

Scott Malone opens the door and looks at Sandra King with a confident smirk. She glances at his plaid bathrobe.

"Nice robe."

He grins.

"Couldn't stay away—could you?"

Sandra turns to look at the hallway.

"How long do I have to stand in your doorway before you decide to be a gentleman and invite me inside your cabin?"

Scott smirks and ushers her inside the room. He closes the door behind her and turns around. He walks over to her.

"Just so you know behind my cocky exterior is a nice guy."

They look at each other for a few seconds.

"Exactly how many girlfriends have you had Scott?"

Scott slowly pulls open his bathrobe so Sandra could see his naked body in its entirety. He looks at her slyly.

"I've been around quite a few times."

Sandra gives Scott a knowing glance and sighs.

"I'll just bet you have."

He laughs loudly.

"What do you want me to say—that I've been a saintly monk—not a chance—I've slept with a lot of women—many of whom were casual one-night stands with no strings."

He rolls his eyes and laughs again.

"OK—I admit it—I'm a dog—satisfied."

"Actually I was wondering if you would be able to handle me. I can be very demanding—lots of pressure for a guy to deal with if he's insecure—and we wouldn't want that—especially since you bragged earlier about your incredible prowess."

Scott rolls his eyes again and smirks.

"I can handle you—no problem whatsoever."

Scott pulls Sandra toward him.

2

Reynolds Estate
St. Thomas
United States Virgin Islands

Nancy Reynolds turns around to face Cole Franklin. He gives her an odd look as he takes a swig of beer. She glances at the checkbook in her hand. He notices and seems annoyed.

"Lady, I've done this before, just relax, OK. Your boy will never know I'm keeping an eye on him—won't ever have a clue that I'm not really part of the expedition. And then later you can decide for yourself when to cut the apron strings for good."

Nancy seems upset by the comment.

"I'll pretend you didn't say that."

Cole rolls his eyes.

"Whatever."

He stands up.

"Time's money—it's up to you."

Nancy reluctantly hands Cole a check.

"I'll call you with updates about your son in two days."

He walks to the door and stops suddenly.

Page 44

"When I get back maybe you'll reconsider about having dinner with me. Heroes have quite the sexual appeal."

Nancy seems aghast and shakes her head.

3

"Yes—everything is going as planned. Bell got the photo from the hidden camera. He's probably looking at it right now as we speak—freaking out royally—and wondering how the fuck it got into his office and who sent it—*who* would dare send it."

Wesley Mayfield grins broadly and nods.

"Uh-huh—their marriage is kaput without a doubt."

He smiles.

"Nobody deserves it more."

He nods several times.

"Yep—I agree. Bell had it coming. He'll get what's coming to him shortly—I'll make sure of it—and enjoy the moment."

He ends the call and smirks.

4

Myles Stephenson looks out to sea as he leans against the railing on the top deck. He smiles broadly as he takes another sip of wine from the glass in his hand. As he turns around he notices the image of an island far away. He shrugs and turns away.

"Nothing there—got to stop drinking."

He looks at the glass in his hand again and slowly throws it into a nearby garbage can. He looks at the container for a few seconds. He shakes his head and begins walking down the hallway. A few seconds later he sees Tristan Montgomery Bell coming toward him. He seems upset about something.

"You and I have to talk."

Myles notices the gun in Tristan's hand.

"Is there something wrong?"

A shot rings out suddenly and barely misses Myles.

"I'm going to kill you."

Page **45**

As a second shot rings out Myles begins running along the hallway in a mad rush as Tristan pursues him. Shots ring out several times and bullets whiz by. As Myles runs past a huge metal cylinder, a bullet pierces it. He's thrown several feet as an explosion occurs. Sparks immediately ignite and flames begin spreading throughout the wood paneling in the hallway.

5

Armand Bell kisses Serena St. John once more and turns to leave. He grins while he looks back at her as he reaches for the doorknob. She strokes his hair sensuously several times.
"You didn't lie about being experienced."
Armand grins.
"I *told* you I was up to the job."
Serena pulls Armand to her and kisses him.
"But are you up to the same job tomorrow and the day after—and the day after that? I like guys with potential."
They share another kiss as he opens the door. Without warning they are met with a wall of smoke. Serena screams.
"*Oh my God*—is the boat on fire?"
Armand immediately slams the door shut.
"What the fuck?"
Serena glances at the window nervously. Smoke can be seen outside as flames shoot upwards a few feet away.
"Where's your cell phone Serena?"
Serena shrugs as Armand begins searching the room in a panic. A few seconds later he finds it and begins dialing.

6

Fire engulfs the top deck of the yacht as Myles runs through a wall of smoke with Tristan right behind him.
"Goddamn you Stephenson. Goddamn you."
Tristan seems confused as he stops and yells loudly.
"I'm going to put a bullet in your head."

Page 46

He coughs several times.

"Got to set an example for sleazy bastards like you who think fucking other men's wives is acceptable behavior."

He fires another shot into the smoke-filled hallway and hears a muffled scream. He laughs loudly in triumph.

"Got you—got the bastard—now to finish him off like I did Fawcett—one bullet in his fucking skull will do nicely."

He quickly runs toward where the sound of a scream came from and falls atop Cooper Johnston. He looks into Cooper's bloodstained face and realizes he shot the wrong person.

"Oh God—*Cooper?*"

Cooper struggles to breathe as he notices Tristan looking down at him with a gun in his hand. Cooper sighs softly.

"Why me—what did I do?"

Cooper gasps several times as Tristan looks at him oddly in shocked disbelief. He shakes his head several times.

"I'm sorry Cooper—meant to kill Stephenson."

Cooper seems to be in shock as he tries to speak. Tristan notices the gaping hole from a wound in Cooper's neck.

"Am I going to die?"

"This wasn't the way it was supposed to happen."

He sighs loudly and looks away.

"I'm so sorry Coop—so very sorry."

A few seconds later Tristan watches Cooper's eyes close and his labored breathing ceases. He glances at his gun.

"I killed an innocent man."

He stands up and looks around seemingly confused.

7
Coast Guard Headquarters
St. Thomas
United States Virgin Islands

Brad McFadden shakes hands with Peter Zimmerman seconds after entering the cramped office. Brad glances at the huge stack of files on top of a desk. He seems disgusted.

Page 47

"After you called I did some checking and the situation with the Hamilton family is just one of many—seems there are cold cases going back as far as 1978—maybe even further."

Brad seems confused.

"How come it wasn't looked into?"

Peter shrugs.

"Not sure—I've just been here for a month—took over the job from a guy named Vaughn—after he had a heart attack."

Brad looks around the office.

"Can we talk to him?"

Peter shakes his head.

"He's in a care facility in Houston."

Peter waves his hand wildly in a sweeping gesture.

"He was stressed to the max."

Brad seems annoyed.

"Seems there's been a slacking of duties—certainly isn't much of a confidence builder if you don't mind me saying."

Peter runs his fingers through his hair.

"Damn rich people are to blame for this mess. Always looking for frigging tax cuts while the country slides further and further into the abyss of a third world society because they refuse to do their part in making for a better situation for everyone."

He looks around the room.

"Cutbacks galore—every month I'm forced to make more cuts because fat cat idiots won't pay their taxes—which fund programs such as these. Bet they don't care one bit that they create chaos everywhere because they want to hold on to their precious wealth rather than help make for a better society."

Brad gives Peter a strange look.

"If they paid their fair share of taxes like they're supposed to—and not be allowed to hide them overseas—programs such as these would have enough money for the hiring of employees to look into cases such as the one pending here currently."

"Lot a good that will do now."

Peter nods in agreement to the comment.

8

Daphne Wade Bell opens the door slowly and is slammed hard by the thick smoke covering the hallway. She coughs and looks around in shock. She begins calling out in a panic.

"Hello?"

There is silence. She calls out again.

"Can anyone hear me?"

She slams the door shut and begins stuffing a few belongings into a backpack as smoke engulfs the cabin.

9

Myles looks back a few times as he hears gunshots in a distance. He sighs loudly and leaps down the stairs—taking two steps at a time. Suddenly there is silence. Myles stops.

"Frigging old coot has totally lost it."

He coughs as smoke engulfs him.

"Fuck."

He looks around.

"Does anyone know there's a fire on board this tub?"

He sighs loudly and coughs again.

"Wonder where the lifeboats are kept?"

He coughs once more and begins feeling his way across the hallway. Visibility is almost non-existent as he bumps into a chair. He kicks it hard and seconds later hears a soft voice.

"Is someone out there?"

Myles stops suddenly and grins broadly.

"Vicki?"

Victoria de Hoya feels her way toward where Myles is standing. She seems relieved to hear his voice. He sighs.

"What's going on Myles?"

They look at each other amid the thick smoke.

"Bell is insane."

Victoria seems confused.

"What?"

Myles shrugs.

"Never mind—we've got to find one of those boats Bell has stored on the side before we all end up as shark bait."

Victoria seems to realize the inevitable.

"Laura."

She grabs Myles by the arm.

"I've got to find Laura."

Myles seems uninterested as he sighs loudly.

"Laura—*Laura Wiley*—my nineteen-year-old daughter is out there—she's here somewhere with a good friend of hers—a pretty blonde—serious print model quality—Diana Munroe?"

"I've met your daughter and her friend Diana."

"You know my daughter?"

Myles makes a lewd gesture with his finger and grins.

"Uh-huh."

Victoria slaps Myles.

"Laura is a kid."

"Not the girl I met earlier—quite a pro between my legs."

Victoria seems ready to slap Myles once more.

"Serves me right for sleeping with you—you charmers are always filthy dogs—but whatever—got to find my Laura."

A loud bang is heard in a distance.

"That was one of the boilers."

Victoria grabs Myles again. They look at each other.

"We have to find Laura and her friend."

Victoria glances at Myles amid the thick smoke.

"There is a flight of stairs right over there. We've got to find my daughter—like right now—before it's too late."

Myles rolls his eyes and shrugs.

10

Armand and Serena reach a stairwell as thick smoke engulfs them. Serena coughs several times as Armand leads the way down the steps. As they are inching their way down they hear several loud voices calling out to them. They answer.

Page **50**

"We're here—about halfway down."

Seconds later they see Amanda Hardwick and Marlene Caswell coming toward them. They seem in a panic.

"Do you guys know what happened?"

Armand shakes his head.

"No—we were on our way to talk to my dad."

Several feet from behind them comes another voice calling out for help. Within seconds they are joined by Diana Munroe. As she is about to speak a boom is heard nearby.

11

"Why are you blaming me?"

Sandra turns to look at Scott with an angry glare as thick smoke engulfs both of them in a narrow metal stairwell.

"I'm not blaming you Scott—I only said if you'd been paying attention we would have known ahead of time."

"Me? Seems we're in this deal together. I don't recall having to twist your arm when I dropped my robe earlier."

"I somehow remember that moment quite differently."

"Typical woman—blame us dudes for everything."

He sighs loudly and coughs.

"*Whatever*—let's just get to the main deck before we pass out in this wretched stairwell. Man, these steps are narrow."

Sandra follows Scott down further as they come to a metal door. He tries the handle. It doesn't budge. He sighs.

"*Fuck*—damn door is locked."

Sandra seems about to freak out.

12

Harley Vanning shrugs as he looks at the open ocean ahead. He glances at a tiny lifeboat lashed against the side of the yacht. He gingerly begins to unlatch the pins that hold it securely in place. As he unlatches the last pin he sees Kyle Bennett coming toward him in a rush followed by a handful of other people.

"Where's everyone else?"

Harley glances at the smoke-filled hallway.

"Don't know—heard some sort of blast and then smoke. I think this yacht is ablaze. Makes sense to prepare the boats."

Kyle rolls his eyes and slowly turns around to look at Armand, Serena, Amanda, Marlene and Diana curiously.

"You kids know how to man a lifeboat?"

Armand nods.

"Somewhat—my dad showed me yesterday."

Kyle looks at Armand suspiciously.

"Think you can handle manning it by yourself?"

"I should be able to. Yeah—I'm good."

He turns to look at the hallway.

"Couldn't find my dad in his office—where the hell is he?"

A shout is heard through the thick smoke.

"Where the fuck is Bell?"

They turn to see Jason Carson coming toward them covered with a wet blanket. He seems very distressed.

"I told that old fool twice we should've done a fire check before we left St. Thomas—and now look at this mess."

Kyle gives him a sour look.

"Let's just get these boats in the water. Then we'll look for the others—this needless chitchat is getting us nowhere."

Jason notices Harley a few feet away.

13

Laura Wiley peeks out from under a hooded jacket as she makes her way toward the railing. As she turns the corner she sees a fiery blaze spreading along the walls of a narrow hallway ahead. She screams and turns back from where she just came. Her sobs puncture the crackling sounds as parts of the hallway behind her falls away and crashes against one of the stairwells. She reaches another stairwell and begins climbing down the narrow steps as more explosions can be heard close by.

14

Wesley looks at the thick smoke permeating the hallway as he reaches the far end of the yacht. He stares out at the open ocean and sighs loudly. As he turns to look at the huge blaze engulfing the front end of the yacht he sees Scott and Sandra running toward him as several large pops are heard followed by collapsing beams. They stop suddenly at seeing Wesley.

"What happened?"

Wesley shrugs.

"How the hell should I know?"

Sandra glances at the ocean and seems frustrated.

"Are there any lifeboats we can launch?"

Wesley gives Sandra a nasty look.

"Like duh—this is a two million dollar yacht."

Scott takes a step forward.

"What's with the attitude buddy?"

Wesley looks at Sandra.

"You better tell your guy to watch his mouth."

Sandra glances at Scott curiously and then at Wesley.

"Why don't you tell him yourself wise guy?"

Wesley looks at Sandra again and seconds later angrily pushes Scott backwards. Scott stumbles but regains himself. As he turns to grab Wesley he realizes he and Sandra are alone.

"Where did that jerk go?"

Sandra shrugs and peers through the thick smoke.

15

Daphne makes her way through the reddish and blue smoke-filled room clutching a huge backpack. She pushes forward as the door opens suddenly. She peers into the smoke but sees nothing ahead. She calls out loudly several times.

"Is anyone out there?"

She's met with eerie silence.

Page 53

Tristan wanders aimlessly through the smoke still holding the gun in his hand as he searches for Myles. He hears voices and stops. He drops the gun as he hears the voices coming closer. Seconds later he sees Scott and Sandra nervously standing in front of him. They seem confused to see him standing there.

"What the hell happened?"

Tristan looks at Scott curiously.

"Do I know you?"

Scott looks at Sandra.

"See, I told you he had memory problems."

Tristan seems irritated by the comment and grabs Scott by the arm. He pushes him backwards as Sandra reacts.

"I've got my facilities intact boy, so don't play games with me. I asked you a question plain and simple. Who the hell are you and what are you doing on my yacht? Tell me boy."

Scott looks at Sandra again and smirks.

"Look at that—he's playing that game again—bet he's not sure where he is right now or that there's a fire aboard."

Tristan pushes Scott backwards again.

"You sneaky little punk bastard—I bet you're a reporter working for one of those trashy supermarket tabloids."

Scott jerks free and backs away.

"No clue what you're talking about old man—but maybe you should care that there's a fire raging out of control."

Tristan begins searching for his gun lying nearby as Scott and Sandra run past him toward the stairwell and disappear in the thick smoke as more screams are heard in a distance.

17
St. Thomas
United States Virgin Islands

Brad watches as Peter waves from a distance and turns to face the open ocean directly in front of him. He sighs loudly.

"Lack of funding—lack of concern—damn it."
He wipes sweat from his brow.
"This is not gonna end well."
He turns again to look at the scene ahead of him.

18

Scott leaps down the stairs as Sandra follows him through the smoke. She stops. Scott reaches an open doorway.
"Come on—that old man is bats."
He sighs loudly.
"We're on the main deck."
Sandra reaches where Scott is standing.
"So, is he right?"
Scott rolls his eyes and smirks.
"It depends."
Sandra grabs Scott's arm and gives him a cautious look.
"Are you a reporter for a trashy tabloid?"
Scott laughs.
"No—*Real Stories* is a respectable celebrity newspaper no different than say, *People* and *Entertainment Weekly*."
Sandra recoils and roughly jabs Scott in the chest.
"*Real Stories* is trash."
Scott rolls his eyes at the comment.
"Hey—a guy has to pay bills. Besides, one man's trash is another man's treasure. Millions of readers can't be wrong."
Sandra jabs Scott again.
"Uh-huh—tell that to the celebrities whose lives have been ruined because of the lies you told about them."
"I don't tell lies—maybe some of the other reporters do but I always tell the truth—which just happens to be bad."
Sandra gives Scott a knowing look.
"I'll bet."
Before he can say another word they hear a yell through the open doorway as Tristan is heard at the top of the stairwell ranting endlessly. Scott shuts the door and follows Sandra.

19

Laura threads her way across the smoke-filled hallway as she hears loud voices. She calls out in panic. A few feet away falling paneling almost hits her. She screams as another piece slips off the wall and crashes to the floor while Scott and Sandra run past her. They stop and turn around to look at her.

"You OK?"

"I think so."

Another piece of falling paneling slips to the floor.

"We've got to get to the lifeboats. Seems help is in short supply around here—feels like we're on the frigging *Titanic*."

He strains to see into the thick smoke.

"Let's go this way."

More pieces of paneling fall nearby with a crash.

20

Deserted Island

A man and woman run aimlessly through a narrow path covered with prickly shrubs as they hear gunshots ring out in a distance followed by a loud booming echo. They stop.

"Think they will send the damned dogs after us?"

Lachlan Hargrove sighs.

"Uh-huh—you and I have to keep moving."

Lindsay White wipes her brow.

"Is there any way off this island?"

Lachlan shrugs.

21

Tristan looks at the gun in his hand and then glances at the ocean ahead. Shouts are heard in a distance. He sighs.

"Where the hell is Daphne?"

He seems disoriented as he walks.

Page **56**

22

Daphne thanks Harley as he lowers the boat into the water. She slowly turns to look at Armand and Serena and someone else she doesn't recognize. Everyone seems in shock.

"Did you see my dad?"

Daphne shakes her head and glances upward.

"I didn't—but I'm sure he's OK."

Armand glances at the smoke billowing from the yacht as another lifeboat is lowered. He turns to look at the ocean.

"Here goes."

As the boat hits the water it rocks a little.

23
Caribbean Sea

Brad looks out at the huge expanse of ocean ahead of him and sighs loudly. He rubs his eyes several times in frustration as he picks up a pair of binoculars lying nearby. He suddenly stops and turns to face a young man standing a few feet away.

"Any word yet from Peter?"

Ben Carlson shakes his head and sighs.

"Zip from Charlotte Amalie. Not so much as a peep in the last hour. I bet he's watching sports or naked chick videos."

Brad seems irritated.

"Bet the damn line is busted too."

He sighs again.

"When I get back, remind me to talk budget issues with Peter Zimmerman—got to avoid messes like this without a doubt if truth be known. This situation is totally unacceptable."

"I agree—will do sir."

Brad turns to look at Ben.

"One more thing—no more addressing me as sir from here on out Ben—no need to use old people formalities—OK?"

Ben seems confused. Brad grins.

"It makes me feel like an old man if I can be brutally honest with someone still incredibly wet behind the ears."

Ben gestures with his hand.

"Like whatever you say."

Brad rolls his eyes at Ben and laughs.

"I'm thirty-nine—really. Still hip and young—got plenty of game left in me. Not ready for the old folks home yet."

Ben laughs.

"Hey, I never said you were an old codger."

Brad rolls his eyes again.

"Never said you did—just want to put it out there that I'm not dead yet—got a few years on you but not by much."

From behind them two other young men in their early twenties poke their heads from around the walkway leading to the back of the boat. They seem worried about something.

24

Scott, Sandra, and Laura reach the deck where Harley is standing, looking over the side of the yacht. They peer through the smoke as he grabs Laura by the arm. She screams.

"You folks ready to abandon ship?"

Scott and Sandra look at each other and nod.

"Are we the first ones off this disaster waiting to happen?"

Harley looks over the edge and shakes his head.

"I dropped a few already about twelve minutes ago."

Laura seems to be looking for someone.

"My mother—classy older woman in her early fifties—did you see her? Is she one of the people you put out already?"

Harley shakes his head.

"Nope—can't say that I have."

From behind them in the thick smoke they hear a boom and then more voices coming toward them. Myles and Victoria reach where Scott, Sandra, and Laura are standing as Harley prepares to lower another lifeboat. Laura and Victoria hug while Myles rolls his eyes as he watches them. He glances at Harley.

Page 58

"Well, how much longer boat guy?"

Harley turns to face Myles with a look of disgust as he motions to Scott, Sandra, Laura and Victoria to climb into the lifeboat hanging just over the edge. Harley sighs loudly.

"Do you want to go down with this ship?"

Myles rolls his eyes knowingly.

25
Deserted Island

Lachlan turns around with a nervous glance as he hears another gunshot in the distance. Lindsay pulls his arm.

"Come on, they're right behind us."

They sprint down several jagged moss-covered boulders.

"Sorry I got you into this mess."

"It isn't your fault—you had no way of knowing."

Lachlan sighs loudly.

"But I still feel."

He points to the ocean.

"I should've known better."

From behind them several more gunshots are heard. The barking of dogs seems louder as panic coldly grips them.

26

Harley jumps into the water and climbs into the nearest lifeboat. He watches as Jason and Kyle look at him oddly.

"What happened to Cooper and Bell?"

Harley shrugs nervously.

27
Fifteen Minutes Later

Four lifeboats drift away from the sinking yacht as several loud booms are heard. Fire engulfs the top deck completely.

"What now? What do we do now?"

Sandra jabs Scott harshly. Waves lap hungrily at the edges of the yacht as it begins to sink below the surface. From one of the other lifeboats nearby Daphne clutches her backpack and seems confused by what is happening before her eyes. Armand looks at the remnants of his father's yacht as it finally sinks below the waves. Serena gently takes his hand. He sighs loudly.

"He can't be dead. He *just* can't be dead."

He rubs his eyes.

"My dad is the toughest man I've ever known. He's not afraid of anything—he always laughs in the face of fear."

They look at each other.

28
One Hour Later

"I think there's an island somewhere out there."

Wesley glances at Myles from one of the other lifeboats with disdain. The putrid smell of smoke is everywhere.

"There is no island around here."

"Earlier I saw something to the south."

Suddenly one of the lifeboats is struck by something.

"What was that?"

"Something hard hit this boat a second ago."

Harley seems panicked as he looks into the mist-covered water. Waves continue to lap silently at all the lifeboats.

"It's probably just something that fell from the yacht?"

Harley's lifeboat is hit again really hard.

"Something is out there."

Waves suddenly churn around the lifeboat.

"Fuck."

Without warning, seconds later several dark objects pop out of the churning waves in unison. As everyone watches in panic from their lifeboats the objects become much clearer.

"Oh my God—*sharks*."

Screams broke the brief silence.

"*We're all going to die.*"

Laura begins screaming loudly in panic as a shark blindly crashes Harley's boat. Kyle stands up and attempts to whack the shark with his oar. But another direct impact tosses him headfirst into the water. His screams echo loudly as he tries desperately to get back into the lifeboat—but as the others watch helplessly another shark circles him. Seconds later he's firmly embedded within the jaws of the large creature. Blood spurts in a massive spray as he is dragged under. The boat is hit again as another shark makes direct impact. It flips over soon after. Jason and Harley are thrown into the churning ocean. Armand reaches from his lifeboat to grab Jason's hand but it proves futile as Jason is pulled under. The mist-covered surface of the water suddenly turns bright red. Serena screams in panic at the bloody sight.

29
Caribbean Sea

Ben looks out at the huge expanse of ocean ahead but sees nothing. He turns around to face Brad and sighs loudly.

"I have no idea how dudes like **Columbus** and **Magellan** did what they did—frigging ocean seems to go on forever."

"Bet they loved every minute of it."

"Columbus maybe—not so much for Magellan—he died violently at the hands of another—probably several in fact."

Ben wipes his brow.

"He must have seriously pissed off the natives in the Philippines royally before they decided to slice him to bits."

"We all have to go somehow?"

Ben shoots Brad an odd look and grins. He mockingly makes a gesture of slicing his throat and begins laughing.

"I prefer later than sooner."

A few seconds later the computer screen in front of them lights up. They look at each other and then at the screen.

"Oh-oh—seems like boat trouble ahead?"

Several more notices appear.

"Think we should check it out just in case?"

"Probably nothing—but yeah, we have to follow up. Bet they forgot to stock up on fuel or something—stupid tourists strike again. Wouldn't be the first time—won't be the last."

Brad heads to the door and stops.

30

"Where the hell did Harley go?"

There is silence as an eerie calm envelops the remaining lifeboats. Through the mist an overturned lifeboat drifts by.

"They got him too."

Amanda notices a dark object coming toward the lifeboats once more. The water churns up again as yet another lifeboat is hit hard by an unseen object. Daphne screams as her lifeboat is rocked by several more blows. She glances at the panic-stricken faces of Armand and Serena as Myles tries desperately to upright the overturned lifeboat floating nearby.

"Watch out."

Myles turns to see a massive fin coming toward the lifeboat. He manages to steer it away. Once the churning water subsides briefly he tries again and manages turn over the lifeboat. From under the boat they see what is left of Harley's broken body. Massive bite marks are clearly visible on the corpse.

"He's dead—*oh God.*"

Attention turns to Victoria as she seems in shock over the sight. Scott puts his arms around Victoria to comfort her.

"We'll be OK."

He sighs.

"Everything will be OK."

From behind them a massive shark appears and viciously grabs what's left of Harley's body and drags it under. Victoria screams again in panic. Two more massive fins appear out of the mists and ram one of the lifeboats. Loud screams erupts.

"We're all doomed. We're going to die."

Seconds later another lifeboat is overturned.

"Grab my hand—quick—OK?"

Myles reaches out to grab Daphne's hand as Armand pulls himself into a nearby lifeboat. Wesley and Serena flail in the water as they watch Daphne being pulled to safety. Armand reaches out to grab Serena's hand as a fin makes its way toward her but misses on the first try. There's no sign of Diana as Serena screams again while Armand tries to grab her hand once more without success. Suddenly Wesley pushes Serena out of the way and tries to grab Armand's hand. Something hits him hard from behind and he tries again to save himself by reaching for the outstretched hand Myles is offering. Screams fills the void as Serena is pulled under the reddish water. Armand reacts.

31
Coast Guard Headquarters
St. Thomas
United States Virgin Islands

As Peter looks at the computer screen in front of him he hears a knock on the door and turns to see his girlfriend poking her head through the door. He smiles. Astrid Blakely opens the door further and nervously looks around. She closes the door.

"Hope you and I are still on for dinner?"

Peter grins.

"Most definitely—I guarantee it."

Astrid walks over to where Peter is sitting.

"Is there any word yet about that missing family?"

Peter shakes his head.

"Nope—total zero at this moment."

He sighs loudly.

"Not even *Nancy Drew* could solve this mystery."

Astrid runs her fingers through Peter's hair.

"I'm cooking something special."

Peter looks at Astrid curiously. She winks slyly.

"OK—OK already. My chef is doing the honors. But he's absolutely top notch talent in case you were wondering."

Peter rolls his eyes knowingly.

Page **63**

"How is Byron?"

"He's fine. He's six going on twenty. Just found out he has several half brothers and sisters and couldn't be happier."

Peter seems confused.

"Explain to me again exactly how Byron ended up being related to one of Maine's richest business families—most notably its elder patriarch who met a tragic end by his own hand?"

Astrid sits down on the edge of the desk.

"To make a long story short, I was acquainted briefly with Howard Madison at a point in my life nearly ten years ago when I wasn't what you would call smart. Anyway, he forced himself on me one night and shortly afterwards I found myself pregnant. Howard and I then came to an arrangement. Not exactly my proudest moment—if truth be known. But I had to do what I could to secure a profitable future for Byron. And now with everything that happened with his family, I think things are better between them and me. They know what happened and decided not to dwell on past events. Next month Byron is flying to Maine to spend two weeks with his older half-brother and his family."

Peter sits up.

"And you?"

Astrid runs her fingers through Peter's hair again.

"Well, if you can get away for a few days I have it on good authority that we can book a vacation to Virgin Gorda."

Peter pulls Astrid toward him.

"And then what?"

Astrid kisses Peter lightly on the lips and winks.

"That depends entirely on you."

Peter grins broadly.

32

"Grab my hand."

Wesley looks up at Myles from the water.

"Don't let those things get me."

Myles tries to grab Wesley's outstretched hand.

Page 64

"When I pull you up, don't look back."

Wesley looks at Myles curiously.

"Why?"

Myles seems annoyed at the comment as he tries to grab Wesley's hand. He notices the water beginning to churn.

"Why do you think?"

Just as he reaches out to grab Wesley's hand, a dark fin appears out of nowhere and grabs hold of its latest victim.

"Oh fuck."

Blood sprays into the water. Myles seems in shock and faces the others. They react in horror as the water turns red.

"Man—look at those teeth chomp away."

He continues to stare at the scene as Wesley's body is ripped to shreds while several other sharks join the attack.

"I hope he made his peace beforehand."

Remnants of Wesley's body float around the remaining lifeboats. Fins appear every now and then before vanishing.

33
Deserted Island

Lachlan and Lindsay run toward a rocky beach from the vine-covered trees. They stop suddenly and listen briefly.

"Looks like the barking stopped?"

Lachlan stares at Lindsay with a worried look.

"They're still out there."

He wipes sweat off his brow.

"Hunting us like prey."

Lindsay notices something in the ocean several hundred yards out from the island. She grabs Lachlan's arm and points.

"Something is out there."

"Let's get a closer look—might be the Coast Guard?"

They run along the rocky beach while looking back every now and then toward the tiny outcropping of rocks where oversized waves crash violently against massive boulders.

As the water around their lifeboats begins to turn red, the remaining survivors begin to paddle away blindly from where they were clustered previous. Sounds of water thrashing about dominate the silence as furious attempts to stay alive become the norm. Suddenly another fin rises out of the mists and rams one of the lifeboats in a raging fury. Loud screams echo loudly.

"Oh God no—*please no*—they'll kill us all."

As Myles watches helplessly he sees the churning water where Wesley was thrashing about seconds before suddenly becomes still. The water is still red. Less than ten feet away he sees Marlene and Amanda clinging to one of the other overturned lifeboats. Seconds tick by like hours. He sighs.

"Come toward me OK?"

Marlene shakes her head.

"They're out there. Those things are out there."

As if hearing her, a massive fin appears. She screams in panic as it glides by her. Myles tries to paddle his way toward Marlene and Amanda. Another fin appears within seconds and attacks. Blood spills into the water in a massive gush.

35
Deserted Island

"Something is happening out there?"

Lindsay turns to look at Lachlan as they focus their attention on several lifeboats adrift in a distance. At that moment a loud boom is heard in a distance—as dogs begin yelping.

"I guess they found my handiwork by the rocks?"

Several more loud yelps are heard in a distance.

"Bet that pissed them off royally."

He wipes sweat from his brow and sighs. Lindsay glances back at where the yelping sounds came from seconds earlier.

"The brothers won't give up without a fight."

Lachlan shakes his head and shrugs.

"I know. But we're not alone anymore."
Lindsay nods in agreement and faces the ocean again.

36
San Francisco

A man nervously looks at his cell phone for several minutes and seems upset. Houghton Fawcett taps his finger on a desk and looks at the cell phone again. He sighs loudly.

"Why doesn't Mayfield respond?"

He glances at several photographs on top of his desk. His eyes fall on a photo of Armand Bell for a few seconds. His vision soon then falls upon a photo of Silas Bell. He begins laughing.

"Bell's troubled eldest son is still locked up in a loony bin in Sydney. Too bad his father has no idea his stupid son outplayed his hand. It would be too bad if something awful happened to dear Silas. He's a sitting duck—just waiting to be eliminated."

He begins to laugh as he rips the photo to shreds.

37

Amanda looks back at the blood-red waves as Myles pulls her aboard the lifeboat. She seems in shock as Victoria reaches out to comfort her. She begins to cry. The other lifeboat pulls up alongside. Armand and Myles exchange silent glances. Armand notices the mist clearing up. He points toward the shape of a small island off to their right as the lifeboats are rammed again from either side. Without a word between them Armand and Myles begin paddling their respective lifeboats toward the tiny island in a distance as two fins aggressively follow them.

TO BE CONTINUED

A Brief Look at the Third Episode

An island shrouded in mystery proves to hold plenty of nasty surprises for a band of survivors who assume their nightmare have ended after a tragic incident at sea claimed several of their own—only to find that there are worst things than death.

Episode 3
Edge of the World

1

"Stop thinking about it—just do it already."
Armand Bell flips his middle finger.
"Easy for you to say—it's not your hand in the water."
Myles Stephenson rolls his eyes.
"*Oh poor baby*—do you want to wait around until they come back—wanting another piece of one of us for lunch?"
As if to answer the question asked, a fin suddenly breaks the surface seconds later and heads toward the lifeboats.
"Oh God—we're all doomed."
"Shut up already."
Amanda Hardwick screams and covers her eyes as one of the lifeboats is rammed. Victoria de Hoya turns to look at the small island up ahead. She sighs loudly and then faces Myles.
"Do you think there are people there?"
Myles shakes his head.
"Doubtful."
Armand rolls his eyes and laughs.
"Like how would he know?"

Armand turns to look at the others and smirks.

"I bet he's spent more time taking crappy photographs that nobody wants than reading maps—if he can read at all."

Myles turns to look at Armand.

"Want to have this out later? I'll whip your ass."

Armand rolls his eyes.

"I wonder how hungry those sharks are right now—might be interesting to find out—use someone stupid for bait."

Amanda begins to cry.

"Enough of the alpha male crap you two."

They turn to look at Victoria.

2

Deserted Island

"I'm so going to enjoy killing those two miserable fools."

Nicholas Harlow kisses the gun in his hand.

"But not before I make them suffer."

He laughs.

"Grandfather taught us well."

His older brother jabs him from behind with the end of his gun as he notices the broken shrubbery less than two feet away. Ethan Harlow stops and inspects the damaged plants as a few eager dogs hover around him. He turns to face Nicholas.

"They can't be that far ahead."

He looks at the gun in his hand and grins broadly as he lavishes attention on it. He strokes the gun lovingly and sighs.

"Got a bullet for each of them—yep I do."

Nicholas glances at the dogs standing nearby with an impatient attitude. He shrugs and looks up at the sky.

"There's nowhere for them to go. Once they reach the beach we've got them cornered. Then our fun will begin."

He glances at the gun in his hand again.

"Damn bastard killed Sebastian in cold blood. He was a fine hunter—couldn't ask for a better dog. *Damn them.*"

Ethan pats his brother on the shoulder.

Page 70

3

"Hit it on the head."

Daphne Wade Bell looks at the oar in her hand as Myles yells at her again. As the shark surfaces again she hits it hard and watches in triumph as it dives once more. A few feet away they see something black rising out of the water. Amanda screams yet again as one of the lifeboats makes direct contact with an ominous object. Seconds later they realize it's just a rock sticking out of the water covered in a tangle of thick black seaweed.

4

Deserted island

Lachlan Hargrove stands motionless as he looks at the strange event taking place several hundred yards out in the ocean. Lindsay White glances back at the jungle as she hears yet another muffled gunshot in the distance and the loud barking of a few dogs. She faces Lachlan again with a worried look on her face. Terrified screams are heard as lifeboats come into view.

5

"Help me."

Everyone turns to look back at one of the overturned lifeboat lying motionless in the water and sees Serena St. John. Armand looks at Myles as Laura Wiley notices a large fin headed toward Serena and screams. Everyone seems in panic mode as it passes by once more. Seconds later it charges aggressively.

"I thought she was dead?"

Armand shoots Miles a dirty look and faces the others with a look of desperation. He looks toward Serena again.

"We have to help her."

Armand looks at the others once more. They seem in shock as they look at him and at Serena several feet away.

Page **71**

"*Right now*—before that thing gets her."

Without waiting for an answer Armand begins paddling toward the overturned lifeboat. Serena nervously watches as the fin surfaces once more. It rams the boat and dives. She almost loses her footing but manages to keep her grip regardless.

"Be careful."

Armand stops paddling and looks at Serena briefly.

"I won't let anything happen to you."

A second fin appears and then a third and fourth as oars rain down on the fins—hitting them hard. Suddenly the water is calm again as Armand finally reaches the overturned boat. He grabs a coil of rope lying at the bottom of his lifeboat and throws it to Serena. She grabs it but seems confused. Armand sighs.

"Hold on to it and we'll pull you behind us until we reach the island. As long as you're on top *they* can't get you."

Serena nods as Armand begins paddling while the others join him. Fins appear occasionally as they move away from the area. Several hundred yards away Myles rolls his eyes at the scene and seems annoyed. He turns to look toward the island.

"Let's hope we make it in one piece."

Scott Malone looks at Sandra King sitting next to him and sighs loudly. He leans over to kiss her on the neck and sighs.

"Are you OK?"

"I guess so."

She squeezes his hand.

6

Caribbean Sea

"All in a day's work for guys like us."

Brad McFadden turns to look at Ben Carlson and grins broadly. They face several people huddled together under thick blankets a few feet away. Ben seems worried and jabs Brad.

"Do you think we got them all?"

"Let's hope so. I'd hate to think we left anyone behind to become chow for hungry sharks—bloody scraps no doubt."

He turns to look at the open ocean and sighs loudly as he starts the engine of the boat. He faces Ben again and winks.

"As as soon as we get back to Charlotte Amalie we've got to find someone who can speak Dutch—these folks probably came this way courtesy of Aruba—quite the trip for sure."

"What about the search for the Hamilton family?"

Brad looks at his watch.

"We've still got enough time to make another swing this way once we drop off our intrepid survivors—an hour or two."

Ben glances at the four people huddled under thick blankets and shakes his head. He slowly faces Brad once more.

<h1 style="text-align:center">7</h1>

<h2 style="text-align:center">Airport Terminal
St. Thomas
United States Virgin Islands</h2>

Cole Franklin sits at one of the airport terminals as he looks at his watch again. He sighs loudly as he taps impatiently.

"That Reynolds chick better deliver on her promise to pay me twice my going rate when I rescue her troubled son. Got a lot of bills to pay and that stingy advance she gave me will only go so far. Got to be able to pay my bills—especially the ones from Royale Casino—can't have those thugs after me—no way."

He glances nervously at his watch again.

<h1 style="text-align:center">8</h1>

<h2 style="text-align:center">Reynolds Estate
St. Thomas
United States Virgin Islands</h2>

Nancy Reynolds nervously looks at her cell phone again before shutting it off. She seems upset as she sheds a tear.

"Why aren't you answering Armand?"

She looks out the window toward the view of Charlotte Amalie in a distance. She wipes away another tear and sighs.

"What's happening out there?"

The doorbell rings. She walks toward the front door and as she slowly opens the carved Mahogany doors she sees a teenage girl standing silently—seemingly upset. She sighs loudly.

"Is Armand here?"

"No—he went on a trip with his dad."

Nancy gives Jasmine Rossmore an odd glance.

"Is something wrong?"

Jasmine looks at Nancy in a pleading way.

"I—I really need to talk to Armand."

Jasmine looks down at her stomach hidden by baggy clothing. Nancy remains silent as Jasmine turns to leave.

"I thought Armand broke up with you?"

Jasmine faces Nancy again.

"We did—*he did*. He wanted to see other people but I didn't. I love him. I've got—I really have to talk with him."

"Do you want to talk to me about it?"

Nancy looks at Jasmine with a suspicious look.

"Maybe I can help?"

Jasmine seems confused as she follows Nancy into the house. Nancy closes the door behind her seconds later.

9
Deserted Island

Lachlan and Lindsay watch from behind a large boulder as a ragtag group of people finally make it to shore. In a distance several fins appear and disappear in the churning waves. Lachlan and Lindsay exchange looks as the little group stop to look toward the thick woods at the end of the beach. In a distance Lachlan hears another shot. Lindsay grips his hand tightly.

"There's no way off this island."

Lachlan cautiously looks at Lindsay.

"Maybe they have a phone?"

"But if the brothers find us before?"

"They won't. I won't let them."

Page 74

"That's what you said before they killed Tim Maynard."

"That couldn't be helped. Tim refused to climb down from the tree when he had the chance. He caused his own death."

"He was scared of the dogs."

Lachlan shoots Lindsay another look at he turns to look at the beach again. He watches as the three lifeboats are pulled out of the waves and dragged toward several large rocks nearby.

10
Coast Guard Headquarters
St. Thomas
United States Virgin Islands

Peter Zimmerman shuts off his cell phone and looks at Astrid Blakely with a worried look. She walks over to him as he sits down at his desk and glances at a stack of paperwork on top with a look of total disgust. He leans back in his chair.

"Are they coming back?"

"Uh-huh—apparently they came across a bunch of Dutch citizens on a pleasure cruise from Aruba. Seems their yacht had some sort of technical issue and they ended up in dire trouble in the middle of nowhere—nowhere being the open ocean."

"Aruba—isn't that quite a ways away?"

"Uh-huh."

Peter looks at the paperwork again and sighs loudly.

"This is unending."

His cell phone begins ringing.

11
Reynolds Estate
St. Thomas
United States Virgin Islands

"Are you sure?"

Jasmine nods and seems about to cry.

"I'm four months along. I took two tests earlier."

Page **75**

Nancy seems in shock as she slowly turns away.

"Have you told your parents?"

Jasmine shakes her head with a look of desperation as Nancy faces Jasmine again unsure of how to handle the startling news she has just been told by her son's former girlfriend.

12

"This is a nightmare."

Myles turns to look at Laura with disdain.

"It beats being shark bait."

Victoria ignores Myles and comforts her daughter as Scott and Sandra glance toward a large grove of trees in a distance.

"How about we check this island out?"

Myles glances at the vine-covered trees.

"There could be things in there with teeth—like really sharp teeth. This island probably has a whole slew of seriously dangerous animals milling about waiting for their next meal."

Armand laughs.

"This is the Caribbean—not Africa—probably the most dangerous thing alive is an iguana—or maybe a werewolf."

"I didn't know werewolves were real?"

Armand turns to look at Serena.

"Uh-huh—heard about them from folks on St. Thomas a week ago at this bar on Back Street. They swear they've seen them lurking in the mountainside late at night—told me never venture out alone after dark—especially in the Mafolie area."

Victoria glares at Armand.

"Stop with the monster talk already—there's absolutely no such things as werewolves—just a bunch of gullible idiots."

Armand winks at Serena.

"Wait until it gets dark and then we'll know."

Victoria shoots Armand another look.

"Does anyone still have their cell phones with them?"

Scott furiously digs his hand into the pocket of his pants and looks at the others curiously realizing his phone is gone.

Page **76**

"I have one."

Eyes immediately fall upon Amanda.

"I have one also."

Laura pulls out her phone but seems upset as she looks at the broken screen. A rush of disappointment fills the group as their attention turns back to Amanda. She sighs loudly.

"I think mine is working."

She tries several numbers but the screen remains blank.

"Nope—it's dead."

Myles looks out at the churning waves.

"It's official—we're doomed."

As he turns away he notices something in the waves.

"Something is out there."

The others look at the ocean and see an overturned lifeboat rolling in the waves. They watch almost as if mesmerized while it comes closer and closer. Several minutes later it reaches the beach. Myles and Scott look at each other and then slowly walk toward the lifeboat. As they get closer they see huge gashes on both sides made by the shark attacks earlier. They sigh.

"It seems pretty banged up."

Scott looks out at the ocean and scans the area for sharks but there are none. He walks closer to the lifeboat and looks back at the group a few yards away. He turns to look at Myles.

"I guess we can use it for shade?"

He turns it over and reacts at seeing Diana Munroe under the boat. Scott and Myles look at each other. Myles sighs.

"Diana?"

Myles shrugs as he seems unsure of what to do.

"What do we do with the body?"

Scott glances at Diana's body cautiously as he gives Myles a harsh glare. He slowly wipes sweat from his brow.

"Doesn't look like she got gnawed by those brutes when the boat flipped—she must have drowned during the attack?"

He turns back to look at the others still standing several yards away. He faces the body once again and sighs loudly.

"This is definitely not my deal."

Scott slowly leans over to get a closer look at the body and realizes Diana isn't dead. He turns to face Myles in shock.

"She's alive."

He faces the others.

13
New York City

Roland Parker looks at the cell phone in his hand and seems annoyed as he shuts it off. He leans back in his chair and looks at the nerdy-looking man sitting in front of him with a stack of photographs. Simon Penney rolls his eyes several times.

"Where the hell is he?"

Roland looks at his cell phone again. Simon stands up. He shoots Roland a nasty look as he glances at his watch.

"OK—I'm done with you—I can sell these really quickly to *TMZ*. Those guys love really sleazy trash—especially when it comes to two straight actor dudes doing it in a bathtub."

Simon is about to grab the photographs as Roland stops him. He hastily scribbles a check and hands it to Simon.

"Sorry—I have other things on my mind right now."

They look at each other for a few seconds.

"I'll be back tomorrow."

Roland nods and watches as Simon leaves. He leans back in his chair again and sighs loudly. He looks at the window.

"If he doesn't call me by tomorrow afternoon I'm done with him. I've had all I can take of his crap. Fuck him."

He looks at his cell phone once more.

14
Coast Guard Headquarters
St. Thomas
United States Virgin Islands

"You saw a flash of light—some sort of explosion?"

Peter rubs his chin as he listens.

"Less than twenty-five minutes ago?"
He sighs loudly.
"Thanks for the info bud—I'll check it out."
He shuts off his cell phone.
"There goes my afternoon without a doubt."
He turns to face Astrid.
"Sometimes I really hate this job."
She walks over to where he's standing.
"I thought that Dutch crew had been rescued safely?"
Peter shakes his head.
"They were."
He slowly sits down at his desk.
"Apparently a local college student with nothing better to do was watching one of those live-streaming satellite videos playing endlessly on YouTube that circle the earth when he saw a flash of light out in the ocean—not far away from the islands."
Astrid seems confused.
"Think this kid is on the level?"
Peter leans back in his chair and shrugs.

15

Diana opens her eyes slowly as Victoria gently wipes her face with a piece of cloth. She seems dazed as everyone hovers around looking at her. Laura squeezes her hand and sighs.
"How do you feel?"
Diana seems confused.
"Where am I?"
Victoria and Laura look at each other nervously.
"We're not exactly sure at this moment."
Laura turns to look at the others standing nearby.
"On an island I guess."
Diana turns to look at the ocean ahead.
"What happened to the yacht?"
"It sank—it happened rather quickly."
"There was a fire on board."

Page **79**

Diana rubs her eyes.

"I blacked out."

Victoria squeezes Diana's hand again.

"Do you remember anything?"

Diana shakes her head.

"Everything is blurred. I remember being in the water and then I felt something hit me. That's all I remember happening."

"You were hit by your lifeboat when it flipped after being rammed by a shark and then you must have floated under it."

Diana's eyes widen with fear.

"I was in the water with sharks?"

Victoria nods.

"It's all over now sweetie."

She looks at Diana cautiously for a few seconds.

"Not a scratch on you."

She glances at the others briefly.

"We're safe."

Diana turns to look at the ocean as Armand faces the dense woods in a distance. Among the dark green and brown of the foliage he notices a few strips of dark blue. He glances at Myles and Scott with a nervous look. He motions them to follow him toward several nearby boulders and then stops suddenly.

"I don't think we're alone."

Armand points at some trees a few yards away.

"I saw something moving a minute ago."

Myles glances at the wooded area where Armand was just pointing and sees nothing. He rolls his eyes and shrugs.

"There's nothing there to see."

Scott and Myles look at each other.

"This isn't the time or the place to freak people out due to your wild imagination. There's nothing there. Except probably some annoying parrot that's sizing us up before mouthing off a few choice bad words someone taught it long ago. Chill OK?"

Armand looks back at the others still hovering over Diana and faces Myles and Scott again. He runs his fingers through his hair several times. Myles sighs loudly and turns to leave.

"Not one more word about this fantasy."

As he turns to walk away he sees from the corner of his eye a flash of blue and freezes. He stops and reacts oddly.

16
University of the Virgin Islands
St. Thomas
United States Virgin Islands

"He probably thinks you're some bozo jerk playing with him. I don't see why you bothered to say anything at all."

John Smythe flips his middle finger at his best friend Boris Birney. Boris reaches out to take a playful swipe at John.

"Next time I broke it."

John rolls his eyes.

"Maybe I should pay him a visit?"

He looks at the computer screen again and sighs.

"It was probably a plane."

He sighs.

"Probably one of those twin-engine deals?"

Boris looks at the computer and grins.

"Or it could have been a UFO?"

John laughs.

"Uh-huh."

Boris sits at the edge of the desk.

"I heard plenty of folks have reported seeing weird lights over the Virgin Islands—sometimes more than one at a time."

John rolls his eyes mockingly at his friend.

"Yeah, I bet they did. Most of the locals have too much time of their hands. Like seriously, some of them think fishing is a sport. Trust me, it's not. Besides—there are no such things as UFOs. If there were, they would have been caught on camera years ago already. No way to hide from video today. Like face it already, people lie, video doesn't. It's that simple—case closed as far as I'm concerned—UFOs aren't real until I see proof."

Boris gives John a push and laughs.

"Like who made you in charge of reality?"
He playfully jabs John.
"You don't know everything."
John ignores Boris and faces the computer again.
"What if the UFO was invisible?"
John shoots Boris a harsh stare and smirks.
"Nice segue to avoid facts but still impossible."
"So you say."
John looks at the computer screen again.

"If there were such things as UFOs out there they would have been seen already. In the past conspiracy theorists had a lot to play with because there were no satellites to prove them wrong, but since the last twenty years or so because of superior advancement in digital technology, it's virtually impossible for anything to enter the earth's atmosphere and not be picked up on video—so there goes the far out stories of stupid farm folks being picked up on some deserted road and probed like sex toys aboard a UFO. Haven't you noticed the freaks that used to talk endlessly about there being intelligent life in those silly 1990s talk shows where everyone was always in a bad mood, ready for a fight, have become less and less talkative? Know why, because even they know that technology will debunk their outlandish tales about "little green men" that even **Stephen King** wouldn't touch."
Boris rolls his eyes.
"*Salem's Lot* is King's best work."
John grins broadly.
"I agree. Read *Salem's Lot* twice. Saw the original movie like ten times. That scene in the cemetery with the dead kid was freaky—kept me up for weeks afterwards with nightmares."
Boris jabs John again.
"No wonder you don't have a girlfriend."
John flips his middle finger at Boris once more.
"Fuck you."
Boris laughs.
"Oops—touched a nerve."
John stands up and walks to the window.

Page **82**

"That was quite a low blow dude."
He seems upset.
"Who do you think you are? **Seth Meyers**?"
Boris watches as John looks out the window for a few seconds and then faces him once more. He seems upset.
"She cheated on me with the football coach."
Boris seems shocked at the statement and slowly walks over to where John is standing. They look at each other.
"I thought you said she wanted to see other people?"
John gestures with his hand.
"She cheated on me a whole month before she told me she wanted to split. Said she couldn't help herself—twisted."
John snaps his fingers.
"She was my first real girlfriend."
Boris watches as John walks back to his desk.

17

Myles rubs his eyes and looks at the thick foliage again but sees nothing. He turns to face Armand with a curious look.
"Maybe we should go back to the others? Best to keep our options together in case not everything is what it seems."
Armand turns to look toward the woods again.
"I told you I saw something."
Armand shakes his head and begins to walk away from Scott and Myles. Scott grabs Myles by the arm. He sighs.
"Should we tell?"
"I don't think that's a good idea."
From behind them they hear twigs snapping at the edge of the woods and turn to see a man and a woman stepping away from several large vine-covered shrubs. Scott and Myles watch as the young couple walk toward them. They wave as they reach within a few hundred feet. From the beach the others also watch silently as the man and woman stop. Lachlan raises his hand.
"My name is Lachlan Hargrove and this is my girlfriend Lindsay White. We've been trapped here for two weeks."

Page 83

Myles and Scott look at each other curiously and then back at Lachlan and Lindsay as they take a step forward.

"Where's here—what's this place?"

Lindsay shrugs.

"We're not sure exactly."

They look back at the dense foliage behind them.

"This island isn't safe."

Myles and Scott look at each other.

"What do you mean by that?"

Before Lachlan can reply they hear a gunshot.

"Are there are other people on this island presently?"

Lindsay nods.

"We've got to hide—like right now."

Myles looks at the jungle-like woods briefly as another gunshot is heard among the barking of several excited dogs.

"What's going on?"

Lachlan glances at the others in a distance.

"There's no time to explain."

Myles suddenly grabs Lachlan's arm and sighs.

"Who's after the two of you?"

Lachlan and Myles look at each other.

"What did you do?"

Lindsay shoots Lachlan a frightened look.

"It's not what you think."

He looks back at the dense foliage.

"We've got to get away from the beach before the brothers get here with their dogs and use us for target practice."

Myles and Scott share a look and motions for Armand to follow Lachlan and Lindsay as they walk toward the others.

18

Ethan looks down at the broken shrubbery just ahead on the trail and stops. He turns to face Nicholas with a grin.

"We'll make an example of them."

He laughs nervously.

Page **84**

"Damn bitch will pay dearly."

He looks at the gun in his hand and sighs.

"Yes, she will."

He strokes the gun for a few seconds.

"I offered to spare her."

Nicholas clenches his fist.

"I told you it was a mistake to trust that whore."

He makes a lewd gesture with his finger.

"I told you she was a she-devil. Grandfather wasn't kidding about what he said about women. Said they're always up to something wicked. Told us that's why he had no choice but to kill our grandmother when our mother was just a very tiny baby."

He wipes sweat from his brow.

"Grandfather said he gave her everything but still she insulted him—insulted his honor—toyed with his affections."

Nicholas glances at the trees again.

"He said she tried to escape with our mother and made it all the way to the lagoon before he caught up with her. Said she left him no choice so he shot her twice in the head and buried her in the crypt underneath the house. Then he raised our mother by himself on this island—said they were really happy at first."

Nicholas sighs loudly.

"Said life was perfect—incredibly joyful."

"Said they got along until she met a shipwrecked sailor that had washed up on the rocks—grandfather wanted to kill him the moment they met but mother fell in love and his life was spared. But then he got cocky and tried to best grandfather one dark night so he was dealt with harshly. Mother found out she was pregnant soon after and nine months later we arrived."

Ethan stops and listens to the silence.

"They must have reached the beach by now?"

Nicholas looks at the sky.

"Plenty of light left to find their sorry asses hiding among the rocks. A couple of bullets and then we can forget them."

Ethan makes a lewd gesture with his finger.

"First time we took her she put up quite a fight."

Page **85**

Nicholas grins broadly.

"Loved your idea of having her boyfriend watch us take turns on his girl—treating her like the filthy whore she is—bet watching us fuck his girl made him nuts several times over."

He laughs.

"I'd love to go another round with her if I could."

Ethan smirks.

"That could be arranged."

His eye catches a curious movement far out at sea.

"Seems another boat met with disaster."

He points to where pieces of wood seem to be floating on top of medium-sized waves. Tiny flickers of smoke can be seen every now and then as the pieces of wood bob up and down.

"Think there might be survivors?"

Ethan looks at his twin brother and laughs.

"Wouldn't make much difference if there were a few plucky survivors—they'll be dead by nightfall if we find them. Unless some of them are women of course. Then they might have a chance to live—at least for a week anyway before we lose interest and use them for target practice on the bluffs."

He laughs loudly.

19
Caribbean Sea

"See anything?"

Ben shakes his head as he faces Brad.

"No sign of any sort of explosion."

"Maybe you're right and that kid was just playing Zimmerman for a chump. I hope he knows he can be traced. Screwing around can lead to really serious punishment issues. I would love to wring his damn neck just for the hell of it."

He shrugs unable to shake his anger.

"Millennials—damn the whole lot of them."

He turns back to face the computer screen in front of him as Ben turns the boat and begins heading back to shore.

University of the Virgin Islands
St. Thomas
United States Virgin Islands

Boris watches as John heads to the door. He stops and turns to face his friend with an odd look on his face. He shrugs.

"Could use the company?"

Boris rolls his eyes.

"Dude, those guys will have you for lunch."

John looks at the laptop in his hands.

"I'm not worried."

Boris walks over to where John is standing.

"I always get into trouble when I'm around you."

Boris points his finger at John.

"For the record I'm broke—like in flat broke—so if you get yourself in a mess with the Coast Guard I can't bail you out like I did last year. You'll just have to be some ugly guy's bitch."

John looks at Boris and winks slyly.

"If he's buying dinner I'll think about it."

"Uh-huh."

They laugh and head out the door. Seconds later the phone on top of the desk begins ringing. It stops suddenly.

21

Myles and Scott gingerly follow Lachlan and Lindsay toward huge rocks while angry waves crash every few minutes all around them. As water sprays continuously they are followed by Armand, Sandra, Serena, Daphne, Amanda, Diana, Victoria and Laura. Every now and then the little group looks out at the ocean as another wave makes its way toward them. Lachlan stops.

"To answer your question about our deal from earlier—we were kidnapped at gunpoint by these two freaky brothers. Said they had lived here all their lives. Our boat initially had a fateful encounter with some rocks on the other side of the island and then as we swam ashore they got us. There were four of us at first—then they killed Freddie Song, Tim's boyfriend when he tried to run away. Lindsay, Tim Maynard, and I were forced to follow them at that point. They beat Tim up, calling him all sorts of terrible names until he could take it no longer and climbed one of the nearby trees. He had nowhere to go and he knew it. They shot him and laughed as he fell out of the tree. Then the dogs ripped him to shreds as he begged for mercy. It was horrible. The brothers Harlow made a show of it without a doubt—told us this would be our fate too if we got clever and tried to escape."

Lachlan watches their reactions.

"They kill people for fun and like doing it."

He looks out at the ocean.

"We saw what happened to you guys earlier."

He sighs loudly.

"Sorry about your friends."

Myles and Scott look at each other.

"Is there no way off this island?"

Lachlan shrugs.

"We heard the brothers talking about a boat hidden somewhere in a lagoon at the western end of the island. I think they use it when they go to St. Thomas or Puerto Rico."

Lindsay suddenly grabs Lachlan's arm in a panicked way.

"What if they're waiting there for us?"

Lachlan nervously turns to face the others.

22
Ten Minutes Later

"This is a bad idea."

John turns to face Boris and smirks.

"We're almost there—quit acting like a girl."

Boris seems annoyed.

"What are you going to do when we get there?"

John nervously glances at the computer lying in his lap.

"I'll show them the video."

"Uh-huh—and they'll show you a cell."

John jabs Boris and laughs.

"I can let you out here if you want?"

Boris glances at John and then at the brightly-colored houses across the street in the Charlotte Amalie suburb of Frenchtown. John pulls over suddenly and smirks. He sighs.

"Well? Do you want to get out here?"

Boris gives John a curious look.

"You can certainly be a fucking prick sometimes."

John laughs loudly.

"It's a family trait from what I was told."

They stare at each other for a few seconds.

"OK—OK—like whatever—let's head on over there and prepare for you to make a fool of yourself. Not that it would be a first—you've certainly been a magnet for trouble of late."

Boris sighs loudly in frustration as John grins. Seconds later he begins driving again—heading into Charlotte Amalie singing a tune. Boris nervously wrings his hands several times.

"I hope you know what you're doing."

He glances out at Hassel Island as they continue driving along the waterfront. Several yards away they notice television cameras being set up facing the harbor. John and Boris turn to look at each other and then back again at multiple news vans with large satellite antennas propped up on top like a beacon.

"I wonder what's going on there."

Boris shrugs.

23
Reynolds Estate
St. Thomas
United States Virgin Islands

Nancy closes the door and seems upset as she leans against the frame. She sighs loudly and glances at a photo of Armand hanging by a large potted plant. She sighs again.

Page **89**

"Hopefully she'll take my advice."

She slowly walks toward the kitchen as the news blares from the television in the living room. She stops to glance at the screen. Flashing stories from CNN about a possible explosion off the coast of the Virgin Islands begin to stream. Nancy gasps in shock as she realizes the possibility. She seems about to faint.

24
Airport Terminal
St. Thomas
United States Virgin Islands

Cole listens as the boarding calls intensify for his upcoming flight. But his attention is riveted to the large monitors in the lobby that begins blaring news about an explosion. As news streams across monitors from CNN and CBS several people stop and look as photos of Tristan Montgomery Bell flash across the screen. Reports begin immediately about the possibility of the disappearance of a yacht and its passengers. On two other monitors nearby, ABC and MSNBC suddenly interrupt their regular broadcasts and begin streaming stories about the disappearance. Photographs of Tristan are shown while followed by a few photographs of Victoria de Hoya. Additional recaps follow as a few anchors begin discussing the de Hoya family.

"Damn it. I thought this was an easy paycheck."

Cole looks at the ticket in his hand.

"Hope that brat is DOA."

He throws the ticket in the trash and heads to the exit of the terminal as more news flashes erupt in perfect sequence.

25
New York City

"This could've been quite the story."

Roland leans back in his chair as he looks at the breaking news on his cell phone. He sighs loudly and seems upset.

Page **90**

"How the hell can a yacht disappear?"

"They think there was some sort of an explosion sir?"

Roland turns to look at his assistant Lance Chang and shakes his head. He leans back in his chair with a blank stare.

"Check your mailbox again in ten minutes. See if Malone sent us anything before he met his end. Maybe he managed to get some photos before everyone were blown sky high."

Lance seems upset at the remark and sighs.

"Quite cold if you ask me sir."

Roland angrily turns to look at Lance.

"But I didn't ask you. Get back to work if you want to have a job when you leave in an hour. Be gone from my sight."

Lance stands up and turns to leave.

"I was only making a point?"

Roland throws a paperweight at Lance.

"*Get out.*"

He turns to look at his cell phone.

26
San Francisco

Houghton Fawcett slams his fist down on a table as he listens to the shrill voice coming from his cell phone.

"What do you mean the yacht is missing? Where is it?"

He clenches his fist and sighs loudly.

27

Waves crash along the rocks as the little group of survivors make their way past massive sprays of salt water and occasional seaweed toward a thin strip of sand-covered beach. In a distance the barking of several dogs can be heard as well as gunshots.

"How far is the lagoon from here?"

Lachlan turns to face Myles.

"We got a ways to go."

Myles turns to look at Lindsay briefly.

"Did either of you see anyone else alive at the estate you mentioned earlier that these two freak brothers call home?"

Lindsay shakes her head.

"No."

She glances at Lachlan nervously.

"They told us all sorts of tales about what their grandfather did in his younger years—mentioned something about him being some sort of Russian count or other—maybe royalty. It was hard to decipher if they were telling the truth."

Scott looks at Lindsay curiously.

"Are you telling me these nutjob brothers are related to the last ruling family of old Russia—one of the **Romanovs**—you know, the ones that got seriously iced during the Russian Revolution when the Communists took over and seized power from the ruling class—then royally screwed everything up."

Lindsay curiously reacts to Scott's use of words and seems slightly confused. She shakes her head and sighs loudly.

"I'm not sure. But I don't think so—probably some distant relative that just claimed to be royalty. This guy they mentioned was their grandfather had a weird name. Count Zaroff I think."

Scott looks out at the ocean.

"How could nobody know they were here?"

Lachlan shrugs.

"I can't say. They bragged about killing a whole bunch of people—some dating back to the early 1990s when they were still in their teens. Said their grandfather lived to be one hundred and twelve. Said he was strong as an ox all his life. Loved killing people for sport from what they said. They claimed he taught them everything. I think they also said he was some sort of a big game hunter back in the day. Built his estate on this island and then caused ships to sink in the rocks off the channel on the other side—used anyone who survived as target practice if they made it to the island alive—they described him as an excellent shot."

Armand and Serena look at each other. A strange look comes across Serena's face. She glances at Lachlan.

"I think I'm going to be sick."

Page **92**

Armand reaches out to put his arm around Serena as he faces Lachlan once more. He takes several seconds to speak.

"Do the brothers have cell phones?"

Lachlan nods.

"I assume. Land lines don't exist this far out from the Virgin Islands. Probably got more than one is my guess."

Scott looks out to sea again.

"You're absolutely sure there's no one else in this island?"

Lachlan shakes his head and seems frightened.

"We didn't see anyone but Ethan and Nicholas Harlow while we were held at the Zaroff estate. If there were anyone else we didn't see them. Not that we would have had a chance to."

He sighs loudly.

"I was tied up the entire two weeks in the basement of their estate—and Lindsay—oh. They were really cruel—sadistic actually—reveled in causing us pain—enjoyed our misery."

He glances over at Lindsay seemingly upset.

"They did terrible things to Lindsay."

He reaches out to hold Lindsay's hand tightly.

"Enjoyed making me watch what they did."

Eyes fall upon Lindsay as several gunshots are heard close by and then angry voices calling for complete surrender.

28
Miami

"Uh-huh—I'm on my way as we speak."

Maxwell Pendergraft sighs loudly as he nods several times before walking toward a ticket booth for American Airlines.

TO BE CONTINUED

A Brief Look at the Final Episode

A search for survivors from the yacht explosion in the Caribbean Sea begin as cable news crews descend in the Virgin Islands en masse hoping for a hot story—while two sadistic killers become determined to kill their desperate prey before help arrives.

Episode 4
End Games

1
Charlotte Amalie
St. Thomas
United States Virgin Islands

Jonathan Vigliotti stands facing Hassel Island as he reports for CBS News while crowds of onlookers stop to watch. A few yards away for NBC News **Jacob Rascon** begin reporting on the same story as more crowds stop and look. Traffic slows down to a crawl as onlookers can't seem to peel their eyes away from the spectacle happening in front of them. Within seconds both broadcasts begin to resemble a Hollywood movie premiere.

2

"Why aren't they calling out anymore?"
Wind whistles through the trees.
"What if they find us before we get to the lagoon?"
Lachlan Hargrove sighs loudly as he faces Diana Munroe standing a few feet away. Her eyes cloud over with tears.

"Best not think about that ending."
Myles Stephenson glances toward the trail ahead.
"I heard dogs barking earlier."
He wipes sweat from his brow and sighs loudly.
"Any idea how many?"
"Ten maybe—could be as many as twenty."
Lachlan turns to look at Lindsay White.

"Neither of us ever knew how many there were—the brothers hid the dogs from view most of the time. I assume there could be as many as fifty. German Shepherds I believe."

She faces Myles and Armand Bell. From behind them Scott Malone rolls his eyes and turns to look at the ocean again.

"Exactly how fucked are we?"
Lachlan shrugs.
"Let's just get to the lagoon as fast as we can."
He sighs loudly.
"Our only chance is their boat if we want to get out alive."
He wrings his hands.
"It's us against them—period."
Scott turns his attention to Sandra King.

3
Coast Guard Headquarters
St. Thomas
United States Virgin Islands

"Oh God—tell me you're joking."
Peter Zimmerman runs his fingers through his hair.
"How did they find out?"
He shakes his head several times.
"OK—OK—keep me updated."
He shuts off his cell phone and faces the window looking out toward the ocean. He seems upset as he sighs loudly.
"How did the news media find out so soon?"
He nervously runs his fingers through his hair.
"What else could go wrong today?"

Page **96**

At that moment there is a knock on the door and he sees John Smythe and Boris Birney standing in the doorway.

"Can I help you?"

John and Boris look at each other.

"I called earlier about seeing an explosion?"

Peter rolls his eyes.

"I'm really busy right now."

Boris glances at John with a knowing look.

"I told you this was a bad idea."

John ignores the remark from Boris and walks toward where Peter is sitting. He slowly pulls out a flash drive.

"I wasn't kidding about what I said I saw earlier."

Peter glances at Boris and sighs.

"Is this some sort of crazy college prank?"

He shakes his fist at them.

"If it is—I'll crush both of you with legal trouble."

"Hey, I'm just along for the ride."

John extends his hand.

"John Smythe."

Peter shakes John's hand.

"The stage is all yours college boy."

He stands up and motions for John to sit down in front of a multi-screen computer. Boris takes a few steps forward and looks at Peter nervously while John pops a silver flash drive into the computer and leans back in the chair. He sighs several times.

4
Waterfront

Crowds gather in front of the ABC News cameras as **Matt Gutman** begins talking to several people while **Ivan Watson** from CNN looks toward the horizon as news continue to filter out about the whereabouts of Tristan Montgomery Bell and Victoria de Hoya. Crowds continue to gather as additional giant screens are set up while a few more news outlets arrive on the scene.

Coast Guard Headquarters
St. Thomas
United States Virgin Islands

As Peter watches, the computer screen comes alive with previously recorded video footage. John's fingers fly over the keyboard as he zeroes in on images of an explosion far out at sea. John's fingers continue flying across the keyboard as the explosion comes clearer into view. He turns to face Peter after a few seconds. He points to the images from multiple angles showing a yacht on fire. Several more images show what appear to be people fleeing in lifeboats. Peter watches in fascination at the footage as he wipes sweat from his brow several times.

"I assume there's a way to see what's happening now?"

John looks at Peter again and nods.

"There is—but it might take a few minutes."

Peter looks at Boris.

"I guess an apology is in play."

Boris rolls his eyes and looks at John.

"No need to."

Peter turns back to look at the screen as John's fingers continue to fly across the keyboard. Suddenly he stops.

"Oh-oh—that's odd."

Peter looks at John curiously.

"What's wrong?"

"Off to the right on the screen there seems to be some huge mass—like a rock or something—maybe an island."

Peter slowly runs his fingers through his hair.

"Must be some sort of huge rock sticking out of the ocean but there's no island that far out—none that I know of anyway."

John leans back in the chair.

"That's no rock."

He points to the screen. Peter leans closer to look.

"Impossible."

John brings the image into focus.

"There's an island out there without a doubt—probably about ten miles or so across—give or take a mile or two."

Peter looks at John curiously and shrugs.

"I've never heard."

They look at each other.

6
Los Angeles

"This could be quite the tale if anyone survives."

Jeffrey Webber leans back in his chair.

"Got a few producers already who would kill for this type of story—tragic tales always excite the public—like *Titanic*."

He turns to face Bruce Mansfield and smirks.

"Free trip to the Virgin Islands."

"Do I have a choice?"

Jeffrey leans forward and grins.

"Not really."

He turns to look at the giant monitor on the wall playing several streams of cable news. He snaps his fingers and laughs.

"Think of it this way—a made-for-cable movie from HBO or Showtime would certainly be intriguing—expensive yacht catches fire in the middle of the Caribbean Sea and aboard are two very important people—one being an adventure seeker who has certainly weathered much scandal and the other is a rich socialite that is an heir to a coffee empire who never worked a day in her life. Can you just imagine the publicity for casting such a potboiler? I can. This will certainly put my agency over the top if we score an agreement with one of the survivors. I'll have calls coming by the thousands every week from name actors."

"What happens if there are no survivors?"

Jeffrey seems in shock.

"There will be. There has to be."

He faces the screen displaying several news channels.

"Go home and pack. I'll have a taxi waiting in front of your apartment ready to take you the airport within the hour."

Jeffrey gestures with his hand and grins.

"This could be our big break."

Bruce stands up and walks to the door. He stops.

"You mean your big break don't you?"

Jeffrey ignores Bruce as his attention seems riveted to the various news broadcasts streaming directly from St. Thomas.

7

Coast Guard Headquarters
St. Thomas
United States Virgin Islands

Peter seems confused as he watches the images from Google Earth coming into view. Huge banks of thick clouds cover the area above a small island as John turns to face Peter.

"That's the best we can get it. Low lying clouds cover most of what can be seen from the satellites that Google Earth uses. It appears that the explosion happened nearby. Possible chance that if there are survivors—they headed toward the island."

John sighs loudly.

"The ocean seems very deep in that area according to the images I'm looking at which usually means the island is subjected to heavy rainfall—which would explain the heavy clouds."

Peter and John look at each other for a few seconds.

"Some of my guys are already in the area."

He wrings his hands.

"Hope to God there are survivors."

He grabs his cell phone.

"I may have to make use of the Coast Guard helicopters."

Boris looks at Peter curiously.

"I didn't know the Coast Guard had copters?"

"We've got two."

John and Boris look at each other.

"Still think I'm a total geek?"

Boris rolls his eyes and shakes his fist at John who turns to look at the computer screen again. Boris glances at Peter.

Page **100**

"Think we'll make the evening news?"
Peter seems annoyed at Boris and turns away.

8
Waterfront

Traffic is completely stalled as massive crowds continue to stop and watch the news coverage as it expands. Several jumbo video screens cover a six block area of the waterfront as hundreds of people seem totally mesmerized by what they see happening. In the water fronting Hassel Island several small boats come into view as well as multiple individuals on sailboats. Within minutes the narrow waterway between Frenchtown and Hassel Island is jammed with sailboats trying to come closer to where the jumbo video screens are positioned. Not long after several food trucks make their way to the area and begin selling food to people standing around. Music coming from nearby cars can be heard as well. On Hassel Island several crafty individuals begin preparing a hot air balloon as they look toward the growing crowds positioned directly in front of the cable news cameras.

9
New York City

Roland Parker looks at the live streaming video playing on his computer and seems hooked on what he's seeing playing out in St. Thomas. He leans back in his chair and sighs loudly.
"Too bad Malone might never see how much of a story he and the others have become. Not even *TMZ* could play a story this well. Got to give it to CBS on this one—this is better than a damn movie from the way they're streaming it. Gone are the days when real news mattered. Throw in a freaky old coot and a coffee heiress and you got the makings of a trashy soap opera."
He begins to laugh as the door to his office opens.
"What the fuck do you want?"
Lance Chang looks at Roland nervously.

"*TMZ* wants to know if you've spoken to Scott yet."

Roland seems about to explode.

"Do I look like I can talk to the dead?"

He stands up and takes a few steps forward.

"Malone is probably on the ocean floor as we speak—of course he hasn't called me—probably never will again. Have they not been watching the news like everyone else? Tell them to go fuck themselves—if they haven't already—which I'm guessing they have judging by what they publish—damn ghouls."

Lance turns to leave.

10

**Reynolds Estate
St. Thomas
United States Virgin Islands**

Nancy Reynolds looks at the news crews standing in front of jumbo video screens and gasps as she sees photos of Armand flashing across the screen. One by one, photographs of all the passengers are shown with their names, while various comments are displayed as well. She slowly turns away from the television screen and nervously looks toward Charlotte Amalie harbor.

11

Caribbean Sea

Brad McFadden peers into the mist with a pair of binoculars and sighs loudly. He continues looking through the thick mist but sees nothing. Low hanging clouds seem to be everywhere. He turns away and faces Ben Carlson standing nearby. He rubs his eyes for a few seconds and sighs again.

"I hope they managed to stay afloat."

Ben looks at the computer screen in front of him.

"I've never heard of an island out here."

"Neither have I. But Peter Zimmerman says differently."

Brad glances at the binoculars again.

Page **102**

"This thing is useless—ancient technology sucks."

At that moment something brushes up against the boat as they look at each other. They head toward the door.

"Wonder what that could be?"

Ben follows Brad to the front of the boat and look in amazement as several pieces of debris float by. Ben sighs loudly as Brad strains to see past the thick mass of dark clouds.

"They're out there somewhere."

He rubs his eyes again.

"I hope they're OK—would be terrible if sharks got a hold of them. Those brutes are relentless once they smell blood."

Ben grins.

"I gather you're not a devoted fan of *Jaws*?"

Brad rolls his eyes.

"Not by any means whatsoever."

Ahead of them they see more debris.

"Something terrible must have happened aboard."

He sighs loudly.

"Tristan Montgomery Bell had a rep."

They look at each other.

"He and his young wife made quite the couple."

Ben snickers.

"Yeah, if you believe they were legitimate."

He smirks.

"Old guy—young woman—gold digger no doubt."

Brad wags his finger at Ben.

"Maybe it was true love?"

Ben laughs loudly.

"Yeah right—whatever."

He makes a lewd gesture with his finger.

"No way that a beautiful young woman would marry a man old enough to be her father unless he was really loaded."

He makes a lewd gesture with his finger again.

"Their sex life must have been abysmal."

He licks his lips several times.

"No way would I marry an old woman."

Brad playfully shoves Ben.

"Bet you'd change your mind if you met the right one."

Ben seems disgusted at the thought.

"I don't care about money."

He winks slyly.

"But I do care about sex—can't seem to get enough."

Brad playfully shoves Ben again.

12

Thick bushes viciously tear at their clothing as Lachlan and Lindsay lead the ragtag band of survivors through dense growths of vine-covered shrubs. As they reach the crest of a small hill Lachlan stops suddenly and faces the others. He sighs loudly.

"The mansion is over that way. And to the north of that is the lagoon. If we can make it there safely, the boat is ours."

He seems worried.

"Except if the dogs find us first."

As if by cue several barks are heard in a distance. A few seconds later several more barks are heard. As the sounds get closer and closer Lachlan slowly turns to look at Lindsay.

"Up ahead is where they first got us."

He clenches his fist.

"Those dogs were definitely not man's best friend."

Loud barks are heard about half a mile away.

"They're getting closer."

About ninety feet away they hear a voice calling out.

"I know you're out there. Give up now before we find you and maybe—just maybe we'll spare your miserable lives."

A single gunshot suddenly rips past them.

"Nowhere to run—it's over—one way or the other."

Several dogs break through the thick brush nearby and begin trying to get at the little band of survivors. Led by Lachlan they begin running along the path as their clothing and skin are ripped by thorny branches. The sound of loud barking echo close behind on the path as several more gunshots are heard. As they

Page **104**

reach another crest nearby they finally come face to face with the lagoon. Directly in front of them about thirty feet they catch a glimpse of a large boat. Lachlan turns around and smiles.

"The path to the boat is just over to the right."

Seconds later a gunshot rips into Serena St. John. Armand reacts in shock as she falls against him. Blood gushes from her chest. Within a minute another gunshot pierces Lindsay's head and she falls backwards into the brush by the edge of the path.

13
Los Angeles

Jared Isling glances at Jeffrey silently. Jeffrey looks up from the folder he's watching. He seems upset and sighs.

"I might have a role for you."

Jared leans back in his chair and shrugs.

"I'm game."

Jeffrey leans forward.

"But you've got to keep your name out of the tabloids."

Jared rolls his eyes and shrugs.

"I have no idea what you're talking about."

"For the record I don't give a rat's ass if you're gay. But I'm not everyone across America. You have an image to play."

"I'm not gay."

Jeffrey throws the folder at Jared.

"Is that so?"

He stands up.

"Your tongue was so far down Peter Zago's throat I'm surprised he could breathe. Stop the "I'm not gay" strategy."

He leans over and whispers in Jared's ear.

"It wasn't just Peter Zago either. You've been quite busy in the last week. Eleven other guys at last count. I'm surprised you had time to go on all the auditions I sent you to. There's nothing wrong with being gay—my girlfriend's sister is gay—but there is something wrong in playing out a lie. People can forgive you for being gay but they can't and won't forgive you for lying."

Page 105

Jeffrey walks toward the window.

"Either come out or keep your behavior under wraps."

They look at each other.

"I don't like having my clients dealing with scandal every other week when it can be prevented. *Real Stories* was bad enough last month but what happens when worst rags like the *National Enquirer* splash your picture with headlines such as *Jared Isling Tongues Buff Stud at Malibu Party*. Your image will be too much of a sad mess to clean up no matter how hard I try."

Jeffrey walks back to his desk.

"I've got one of my writers putting together a treatment covering that tragic incident happening in the Virgin Islands."

Jeffrey smirks.

"You could play Scott Malone."

Jared reacts with disgust.

"Isn't he the one who wrote that story about me?"

Jeffrey nods.

14
Caribbean Sea

"Ugh."

Brad slowly retrieves the remnants of a human hand in a net. He turns to face Ben as they look at the grisly scene. Ben seems about to throw up as he turns away from the net.

"I guess we don't have to wonder."

He watches as Brad drops the remains into a box.

"According to Zimmerman the island is about a mile to the right. Said it was covered in clouds—dark paradise without a doubt—certainly not the place to book a summer vacation."

Ben rolls his eyes and stares blankly at the box for a few seconds. Brad notices Ben's reaction and cracks a smile.

"I could bring it closer for a better look?"

Moments later several other crew members come toward them with additional pieces of mangled human remains.

15
Coast Guard Headquarters
San Juan, Puerto Rico

Two helicopters take off in unison and head toward the open ocean as Pedro Mendez and Jason Varley wave. They watch until the humming sound trails off and the helicopters vanish from view. As they turn back toward the helipad they see several men in expensive suits headed toward them. Pedro sighs.

"I wonder who those guys are."

"We're about to find out."

They walk towards the men in expensive suits.

16
Hoya Coffee Corporate Offices
San Juan, Puerto Rico

The lobby is filled with reporters as several people walk back and forth while talking on cell phones. They stop every few seconds to glance at the gaggle of reporters seemingly becoming less and less patient as time slips by. Alexander de Hoya steps out from a side office and slowly comes toward one of the reporters nearby talking on a cell phone. He whispers in their ear.

17

Laura Wiley screams as another bullet rips through the bushes nearby. A second bullet whizzes past them. Less than a minute later Diana feels something rip through her blouse. She reacts in shock as she realizes it only grazed her. But suddenly another bullet finds it mark in Amanda Hardwick. She falls backwards. Blood spurts out of her chest in a massive spray.

"Can we still make it to the lagoon?"

Armand turns to look at Myles with disdain as they hear dogs barking nearby. The sounds seem much closer.

"Is your personal safety all you can think about?"

Several dogs break through the thick brush and begin making their way toward the band of survivors. Right behind them Ethan Harlow appears. He brandishes his gun proudly and seems somewhat stunned to see the others. He grins slyly.

"Well, well, well. What do we have here?"

He looks at Lindsay's body.

"Hello Lachlan."

Ethan looks at the dogs standing at his side. They seem to be waiting for a command. He grins broadly and takes another step forward. An odd silence befalls the area briefly as moaning sounds can be heard. Ethan looks at Amanda and upon realizing she's still alive, aims his gun at her and shoots. He erupts in laughter as he looks at the bullet sticking out of her forehead.

"She was dead anyway."

He turns to face the others.

"Who's gonna be next?"

From behind him Nicholas Harlow steps out of the brush and stares at the scene slightly amused. He notices Lindsay's body and smirks. He and Ethan exchanges looks. He sighs.

"Lachlan made some new friends I assume."

Ethan grins broadly as he looks at his gun again.

"These must be from that explosion we heard earlier."

He watches as Nicholas glances at the dogs.

"Should we give them a few seconds to get to the lagoon just to be fair? See if they can actually make it? Should we?"

They laugh and point at Lachlan.

18
Caribbean Sea

Brad looks toward the outline of the island up ahead and sighs loudly. He seems unsure of what to do next. Mist permeates the area but most of the clouds seem to be dissipating as the boat reaches within about three hundred feet of the island. Several large black rocks can be seen protruding from the water.

"Damn place is riddled with death."

"Got all the remains I assume?"

"There's probably more that'll show up later—must have been a sweet feast earlier. The grim reaper certainly was busy today. The water still seems stained with blood. Terrible."

From above they hear loud sounds as two helicopters with specially-equipped ladders come into view. Ben grins broadly.

19
Coast Guard Headquarters
San Juan, Puerto Rico

"We're doing everything to rescue your sister."
Pedro looks at Samuel de Hoya.
"We just sent out two helicopters fifteen minutes ago."
Samuel nods and faces Milo Wiley.
"This is Victoria's son."
They look at each other.
"We're here to offer assistance if needed."
"Much appreciated."
Milo glances at several news crews in a distance.
"What about them?"
"We tell them nothing for now."
He glances at two other men standing nearby. Samuel turns to face them and motions they come forward. They extend their hands just as Jason notices his cell phone flashing.

20

"You'll never get away with this."
"We'll see."
Nicholas glances at Lachlan.
"We're in the middle of nowhere. No one knows you're here. No one will miss you. Your deaths won't even matter."
He points his gun at Scott and Sandra.
"Seems to me this is as good a time to begin target practice—thin out the herd—make things more exciting."

Page **109**

Before he can fire, loud sounds are heard far above. A few seconds later two large helicopters come into view. Clearly visible on the side are the words UNITED STATES COAST GUARD. As Ethan and Nicholas look up, Victoria de Hoya pulls out a tiny object from a pocket in her slacks and watches with glee as the dogs standing nearby begin to whimper in pain—scratching their ears. Instantly the remaining band of survivors begin running toward the lagoon. Ethan and Nicholas join in pursuit leaving the dogs behind crying painfully. From above several ladders stream down as armed individuals make their descent into the island.

21
Coast Guard Headquarters
St. Thomas
United States Virgin Islands

"This is totally fantastic—like a movie—but real."
John glances at Peter and grins broadly as he looks at the streaming video coming directly from above a small island. They watch the scene playing out as one of the helicopters begins unfurling several chain-link ladders into the jungle far below.

22
Waterfront

As the crowds continue looking eagerly at the jumbo video screens broadcasting the latest updates, there is a blip and suddenly footage showing two very large helicopters hovering over a small island in the Caribbean Sea begins streaming with what looks like men and women climbing down ladders into a jungle as clouds obstruct their view every now and then. As everyone watches in fascination, more ladders are unfurled and what appears to be about fifty more individuals making their way into a jungle far below. Crowds break out in loud cheers while several reporters begin to interview those standing around.

Myles jumps over several rocks as he makes his way toward the lagoon. Armand, Daphne Wade Bell and Diana follow close behind as Victoria and Laura make their way down another part of the embankment. Lachlan, Scott, and Sandra climb through another opening in the rocks as they see Ethan and Nicholas following them in close pursuit. High above, the roar of two large giant helicopters echo loudly. Myles jumps into the lagoon and heads toward the boat while Armand and Diana stand on the edge seemingly wondering what to do next as several gunshots are heard. Daphne runs into the lagoon after Myles as Victoria and Laura finally reach where Armand and Diana are standing. At a distance Lachlan, Scott and Sandra can be seen running toward the others when a single gunshot rings out as birds scatter. Lachlan falls into the lagoon face first. Blood spurts from a hole in his head. Scott and Sandra seem in shock for a few seconds and then begin running along another path toward the lagoon. More shots ring out as Ethan and Nicholas begin shooting wildly—trying in vain to hit one of the others. As Daphne reaches the boat two shots ring out loudly. She screams in pain.

"It's over bitch—you lose—I win."

Nicholas shoots Daphne fatally and she topples into the lagoon. He fires several more shots—hitting her again in the head. As her body sinks beneath the water he faces Myles.

"Say your prayers."

He fires several rounds at Myles. One of the bullets hit the gas tank and the boat explodes into a fireball. Myles is burned alive within seconds. Ethan and Nicholas share a sly grin.

"Grandpa would've been so proud."

They turn around and face the others. There is a hushed silence as moments seem like hours while seconds tick by.

"I bet you didn't think it would end like this?"

"None of you are going to get off this fucking island alive."

Nicholas aims his gun at Scott and Sandra.

"*Drop your weapons—we've got you surrounded.*"

Ethan and Nicholas turn around to see about fifty armed individuals looking at them. They slowly look at each other and again at the remaining survivors standing a few yards away.

"I won't ask again."

Ethan and Nicholas look at each other again.

"Fuck you."

As Ethan raises his gun he's shot several times. His skull shatters as bullets tear into it. As Nicholas looks at his brother's broken body he attempts to shoot Diana. Multiple bullets rip into his body as blood sprays everywhere. Seconds later it's over.

24
Waterfront

Crowds cheer wildly as the images on the jumbo video screens continue to stream live. As they continue cheering, a boat approaches the lagoon on the island. Brad and Ben can be seen signaling the helicopters above as they pull into the lagoon.

25
Coast Guard Headquarters
St. Thomas
United States Virgin Islands

John shakes Peter's hand and turns to look at Boris standing at the door. He sighs loudly and faces Peter again.

"I'm glad I could help."

"Without you none of what happened would be possible."

He glances at the computers nearby.

"Tomorrow eight o'clock sharp—no excuses."

John nods in agreement. As they close the door and begin walking down the hallway Boris looks at John and smirks.

"Think they'll make this into a movie?"

"If Hollywood can make a movie about a drug-addicted homeless guy who turns his life around because of a cat I'd say this story definitely has movie potential written all over it."

Boris playfully jabs John and sighs.

"*A Street Cat Named Bob* was a good movie."

John stops and faces Boris. He wrings his hands.

"I agree. **Bob the Cat** even played himself perfectly in the movie—and the actor who played the drug addict was great too. **Luke Treadaway** nailed the role—made it look so easy."

They reach the entrance of the building.

26
Reynolds Estate
St. Thomas
United States Virgin Islands

Nancy clasps her hand over her mouth as she watches the live footage coming from the island. Her eyes cloud over as she catches a glimpse of Armand being led through a path toward a chain-link ladder. She sighs loudly as she sees him beginning to climb upward into a helicopter hovering about forty feet above the thick growth of trees. Her eyes fall on Diana and Laura as they follow Armand and begin climbing upward while Victoria is seen being led toward the chain-link ladder as several bodies covered with white sheets are loaded onto stretchers about ten feet away. A short distance away she sees Scott and Sandra talking to a few armed men and then they too are led toward the ladder.

27
San Francisco

"Sad that Wesley Mayfield didn't make it."

A man looks away from live streaming video as he leans back in his chair. He smirks as he looks at a photograph of a handsome young man. He gently rubs his eyes a few times.

"He was so dedicated."

He seems visibly upset and sighs loudly.

"Mayfield was like a son to me."

Houghton Fawcett shrugs and then laughs.

"I wish I had been there when Bell saw the photo. That lousy bastard deserved everything he got. Finding out his young wife was fucking Stephenson was sweet revenge. It was genius of Wesley to put a hidden camera in Stephenson's room."

He looks at the photo of the handsome man again.

"Ralph wasn't perfect by any means and he could've used better judgment when it came to Bell's wife. But your brother didn't deserve to be murdered. Once it became clear Ralph was dead I had to act. I had to even the score. Mayfield came highly recommended, an excellent private investigator without a doubt. Bell never knew he was being played. Tristan Montgomery Bell is at the bottom of the Caribbean Sea at this moment. I hope he suffered before he kicked the bucket. Damn him to hell."

He faces Loren Fawcett sitting in front of him.

"Tomorrow I'll take control of Bell's precious holdings."

Loren nods in agreement and stands up.

Two Days Later

28

Brad looks at Maxwell Pendergraft in dismay and sighs as hundreds of mummified human remains are brought out from a large room—many of which are in various stages of decay. As the final mummy is removed Maxwell seems to recognize the body as it is placed onto a glass container. He faces Brad and sighs.

"Sanger Rainsford."

He watches as the container is carried toward the lagoon.

"According to Rainsford's great granddaughter who lives in Philly—he disappeared in 1924 on a trip to the Amazon. She said her family always wondered what happened to him."

He shakes his head.

"His parents went to their graves wondering."

From a crypt nearby they see several caskets being brought out. Maxwell runs his fingers through his hair as he seems in shock at the grisly scene playing out in front of him.

"Count Zaroff certainly will have a place in the annals of true crime narratives. He makes **Jack the Ripper** look like a Sunday school teacher by comparison. His grandsons certainly made every effort to carry forward his vile, dark legacy."

Two more caskets are carried away.

"Once the crypts are completely emptied the mansion will be torn down and the island will officially become a public park managed by the National Park Service. Plans are underway to have it patrolled regularly to keep possible copycats away."

"What's going to happen to the bodies?"

"We've already begun trying to find relatives of the departed—either on the mainland or in Europe. Until then everyone will be reburied on St. Thomas in a private vault."

Several men with gloved hands come toward Brad and Maxwell and begin pointing at two remaining caskets as they are carried away. Brad wipes sweat from his brow and sighs.

"Count Zaroff and his wife I presume?"

They nod and silently walk away.

"That's the last of the bodies—might as well get the demolition guys ready to start the second phase of this story."

Maxwell immediately pulls out his cell phone.

One Week Later

29

John and Boris smile broadly as photographers snap wildly while they shake hands with Armand, Scott, Sandra, Diana, Laura and Victoria. Behind them video cameras stream footage to a worldwide audience as crowds nearby cheer. Headlines at the bottom of the screen comment several times on the fact that a movie is being planned based on the rescue as well as the story about the tragic Zaroff murders dating back over a century.

About the Series Creator

Gary Brin was born in 1965 and has lived in the United States Virgin Islands, Hawaii and California. He has edited numerous original literary works over the years—both new and revised. In 2019 he established Standish Press to bring forth interesting fictional and historical material usually ignored by mainstream publishers because of specific views or content. In addition to publishing books, he also created the Nancy Hanks Lincoln Public Library (named after the mother of Abraham Lincoln) in 2014 to make available hard-to-find books to a worldwide audience.

Production Notes

Written by Wesley Adams and Daphne McGee
Manuscript edited by Gary Brin
Cover photograph from www.pexels.com
Front cover design and interior book layout by Gary Brin
Cover layout by Victoria Valentine
Additional help provided by Carlton J. Young
Series created by Gary Brin

Character List

Armand Bell
Daphne Wade Bell
Tristan Montgomery Bell
Kyle Bennett
Boris Birney
Astrid Blakely
Ben Carlson
Jason Carson
Marlene Caswell
Lance Chang
Alexander de Hoya
Samuel de Hoya
Victoria de Hoya
Houghton Fawcett
Loren Fawcett
Cole Franklin
Amanda Hardwick
Lachlan Hargrove
Ethan Harlow
Nicholas Harlow
Jared Isling
Cooper Johnston
Sandra King
Scott Malone
Bruce Mansfield
Jennifer Marlowe
Wesley Mayfield
Brad McFadden
Pedro Mendez
Diana Munroe
Roland Parker
Maxwell Pendergraft

Simon Penney
Nancy Reynolds
Casey Roberts
Jasmine Rossmore
John Smythe
Serena St. John
Myles Stephenson
Harley Vanning
Jason Varley
Jeffrey Webber
Lindsay White
Laura Wiley
Milo Wiley
Peter Zimmerman

Real People and Animals Mentioned

Bob the Cat
Christopher Columbus
Matt Gutman
Jack the Ripper
Stephen King
Ferdinand Magellan
Seth Meyers
Jacob Rascon
Romanov Family
Alexander Skarsgard
Myles Standish
Luke Treadaway
Jonathan Vigliotti
Ivan Watson

Next in the Series
Book 4
Thomas Nix